The Important Question

What could she do to make up with Wendy? That was the important question. She had to do something because it was a lonely, dreary world without her. Wendy always had something exciting to talk about, always a fun scheme planned. Every morning Jessica woke up looking forward to the day because Wendy was there. It was impossible to think of life without Wendy. What would she do? What would she think about? What would she say?

Also by Marilyn Sachs

A Secret Friend

By
Marilyn Sachs

AN
APPLE
PAPERBACK

SCHOLASTIC INC.
New York Toronto London Auckland Sydney

Handwritten notes by
Catherine Greenman, Edward Greenman,
Brad Lauren, Robert Phillips,
Jane Reilly, and Tony Reilly.

ISBN 0-590-40403-2

12 11 10 9 8 7 6 5 4 3 2   7 8 9/8 0 1 2/9

Printed in the U.S.A.   11
First Scholastic printing, February 1987

Remembering all the friendships
my family and I made there,
this book is affectionately dedicated
to the students and staff,
past and present,
of Cabrillo School, San Francisco

A Secret Friend

Chapter One

Wendy Cooper is not your
friend. She talks about
you behind your back. You have
a better friend in this class.
A.S.F.

T he note lay folded on Jessica Freeman's seat
when her class came back from gym. It had
a large J.F. on the outside. The handwriting was un-
familiar, sloping left, obviously disguised.

Jessica's cheeks flushed as she read it. She could
feel a nervous pulsing in her throat, and she looked
eagerly around the classroom. Nobody was looking in
her direction. She read the note over and over again,
standing above her seat, frowning, wondering what
next.

"Jessica," said Mr. Prince finally, "I don't mind
people passing notes back and forth, as I've told the

class many times, but I was hoping to show a film on killer whales during the next period. I wouldn't want to turn out the lights while you're reading your note —for the eighth or ninth time I would guess—so if you would just let me know when we might begin, I would be very grateful."

Her cheeks burned as she heard the laughter rising around her. Wendy's high hyena laugh was the loudest. Mr. Prince thought he was so funny! All the kids were looking at her, laughing, all the kids, she noticed, except for Randy Jackson. He had his eyes down on his desk and was frowning. Randy Jackson? What about him? Later she'd have to figure it all out but now she sat down quickly, folded the note, and tried not to look embarrassed.

While she was eating her lunch, alone, out in the schoolyard, Wendy came and sat down next to her. "Who was that note from?" she asked.

Jessica kept her eyes on Randy. He had finished lunch, and was playing kickball. His team was out in the field, and he was pitching. He stood motionless, now, tall and slim and handsome in his well-fitting jeans and bright red cord shirt. Lori Chu was up, and you could just see how Randy was psyching her out. Lori fidgeted at home plate, and Randy took a hard look at her, crouched, and threw. Lori kicked the ball hard—right in his direction, high, over his head, but he leaped up, straight as an arrow, and caught it effortlessly.

"Who was the note from?"

2

This was the first time in days that Wendy had sat down next to her during lunch. Be cool, Jessica said to herself, friendly but cool.

"How come you're sitting near me all of a sudden?" she said, and knew it was the wrong thing to say.

"Don't start that again," Wendy said.

Be cool, Jessica told herself. This is your chance. "It's only because Barbara's absent, right?" There was a whine in her voice that she hated. There was often a whine in her voice when she spoke to Wendy.

"As a matter of fact, you're right," Wendy said coldly, and stood up. "I guess I'll go and do something interesting."

"Wait!" Jessica said desperately. "Don't go! Don't you want to know about the note?"

"Oh, yeah! That was really funny when Mr. Prince said he wouldn't think of putting out the lights when you'd just read the note only twelve or thirteen times. Boy, were you ever embarrassed!"

"Eight or nine times," Jessica corrected, watching Wendy laugh, showing her large, long teeth, and wondering how she'd look if she read the note. Should I show it to her, Jessica wondered.

"Well?"

"Well what?"

"Who was the note from?"

Jessica shook her head. "It didn't say."

"Well, let me see it." Wendy held out her hand and Jessica hesitated. Wendy was still laughing, so that decided it. Jessica handed her the note, and watched her face change as she read it. That big, toothy laugh froze when she got to the part about herself. Suddenly, she looked like a jack-o'-lantern.

Watching Wendy's face, Jessica wondered why it was that you could hate someone as much as she hated Wendy, and still want to be friends. Ever since their friendship began, it seemed to Jessica that there were always more things that she hated about Wendy than liked. Wendy was mean. She was always playing tricks on people or thinking up insults, like with Susie Edelstein. Jessica might laugh—she always did laugh sooner or later—but underneath she recognized the meanness, and was afraid of it. Wendy never admitted she was wrong. In the past, whenever they argued, Wendy always said it was Jessica's fault. She could stay angry for days and days. Jessica couldn't. Jessica hated having people angry at her, hated feeling shut out by cold, tight faces. She always ended up apologizing to Wendy even when she wasn't sure what she was apologizing for. She hated saying she was sorry for something she had never done, and she hated Wendy for making her do it.

In most of the books that she read a person was either bad or good, but life wasn't like that. Wendy was mean, but she was also fun and exciting to be with. She might tease one minute but the next minute she would listen to your complaints and sympathize. She might make fun of you and imitate the way your teeth stuck out but later she might also comb your hair into a new style, and crown you with a tiara of paper clips.

"A.S.F.?" Wendy said savagely, "I'll bet I know who that is."

"Who?" Jessica asked, her eyes on Randy as he rounded third base on his way home.

"Anita. She's so jealous of me, any chance she gets she'll do something mean."

"But Anita's last name is Loomis, and I don't know what her middle name is," Jessica protested. "I'm sure it's not Anita."

Wendy was studying the note. "It's got to be some weirdo," she said. "That I know for sure."

Be cool, Jessica told herself, cool and careful. "Well," she said, wondering if Wendy could hear the thumping in her chest, "what do you think—I mean —the part about you?"

"I think," Wendy said, looking hard into Jessica's face, "that this is from a weirdo, and that you've been opening your big mouth about me all over the place."

"Me!" Jessica cried.

"Yes, you, all over the school. Everybody knows any time we have an argument or I don't sit near you at lunch or if I take a bite out of Barbara's baloney sandwich but not yours—you gotta blab all over the school."

"No," Jessica cried. "I never blab. I keep it all inside. But you're the one—you tell everyone that I have cooties, and that I'm a baby, and a . . ."

5

"Oh, shut up!" Wendy commanded, fluttering her hand contemptuously in Jessica's face. "All you ever do is whine. Well . . ." She studied the note and wrinkled her forehead. "If it's not Anita, then who? Hmm. A? What about Alan?"

"No, his last name is Rogers. It can't be him."

Suddenly they were confederates. Jessica licked her braces, and moved in a little closer.

"A.S.F. . . . ? Hey, I know."

Her blue eyes had such a friendly, sharing look that Jessica smiled, and Wendy smiled back. There, it was all over, and they were friends again.

"Susie Frankel? See—the A is nothing, but S.F.— that's her initials. I'll bet she's the one. What do you think, Jess?"

They were close now, whispering, weaving their own magic circle around themselves. Like old times. Back together again! Jessica could smell the egg salad on Wendy's breath.

"No," she smiled into her friend's smile, "it's not Susie. It can't be. But, Wendy, can you come over this afternoon?"

Wendy stopped smiling. "Why not? Why can't it be Susie Frankel? She's a real turkey, and she hates my guts."

"Because she's absent today. Anyway, maybe A.S.F. isn't a person's name. Maybe it means something else. But, Wendy, how about this afternoon?"

"Maybe you know who it is, and you're just not saying," Wendy said, pulling back out of the circle.

6

"No, no," Jessica cried, "I don't know who it is. Come on, Wendy, let's forget the note. Can you come over today?"

"No, I can't—and who cares about your stupid note anyway." She pushed the note at Jessica, jumped up, and started walking away.

It was all over again and why? What had happened? What had gone wrong this time?

Quickly Jessica called after her, "Well, maybe it is Susie Frankel. Or maybe—wait Wendy, how about tomorrow? Can you come over tomorrow?"

"I've got a piano lesson tomorrow. You know that!" Wendy called back over her shoulder, still moving away.

"Well—Wednesday—Wendy—Wednesday?"

Wendy stopped and turned. She was wearing a long strand of blue glass beads, and she fingered it as she looked back at Jessica. It was a look that Jessica had experienced in the past—a terrifying look—one that was teasing and watchful at the same time. Wendy was standing there waiting. Waiting for what? Wendy was standing there, touching her blue beads and waiting. Then Jessica knew.

"Wendy!" she howled. "You're not wearing it."

"Not wearing what?" Wendy stroked her beads slowly.

"Your poison locket. Oh, Wendy, you're supposed to wear it every day."

"I don't want it any more. I gave it away." Wendy continued stroking her beads, but now she was watching Jessica, and smiling, showing her large teeth.

"Gave it away?"

"Yes," Wendy said pleasantly. "I gave it to Barbara." She remained standing there, fingering her beads, smiling, waiting.

What was there to say? Jessica could feel the hatred radiating out from behind that smile. She sat down, and turned away her head. She wasn't going to cry in front of Wendy. She waited until she heard Wendy moving off. Then she took a deep breath, and tried to blink back her tears. What had happened? Why had it happened? One day, she and Wendy had been best friends, had been sitting together at lunch, walking to and from school every day, filling up nearly all the spaces in each other's lives. Best of all, for Jessica, there had been for over five years now that charmed circle that surrounds every pair of best friends. Inside it, you are safe and snug and happy. Outside it, you are helpless and exposed.

She put up her hand, fingering her own poison locket, and remembering the Christmas before last when they were in the third grade. She and Wendy had bought identical gold-plated lockets at Wiggett's jewelry store with their Christmas money. It was Wendy's idea to keep powdered Jello inside, and tell everybody it was poison. Joanie Lucas had cried her head off one day when they showed her how she'd eaten a graham cracker sprinkled with poison.

None of the kids believed them any more about the poison, but everybody knew that they both wore their lockets every day and slept with them on at night. For nearly two years now, they had worn those lockets every single day without fail. All the kids knew that the lockets meant they were best friends.

Best friends!

All around the schoolyard, clumps of kids talked and played together. I am all alone, Jessica thought. She closed her eyes, and thought about dying.

Suddenly a sharp pain in her chest slammed her against the school wall. She opened her eyes, and there was Randy rushing toward her.

"Oh, Jessica, are you all right?"

She began crying, her tears were as much from relief at being alive, as from pain at being hit by a ball. Randy was there then, helping her up, questioning gently, "Are you all right? I'm sorry, Jessica, I really am. Are you all right?"

Her face was buried in her hands, but she could feel a crowd of kids around her. "Is she all right? What's wrong? Take her to the office."

"Do you want to go to the office, Jessica? Come on, I'll take you." Randy's arm was around her shoulder, and she shook her head finally, looked up at him, and said, "I'm okay, Randy. It's all right."

"You sure?" His dark eyes were concerned and troubled. She nodded, smiled and he smiled back.

"Well, okay then."

He was off again, back to home plate. She saw him pause, turn again toward her, wave, and then poise for the pitch.

"Randy?" Well, why not. He'd be perfect for

A.S.F. She thought of her note and fingered her locket. Carefully, coolly, she put her hands around her neck, unclasped the locket, carried it over to the nearest garbage can, and tossed it in. If Wendy could get rid of her locket, well so could she. Two could play that game just as easily as one. She looked over toward Wendy to see if Wendy had noticed, but Wendy was arm wrestling with Peter Fink.

Still, Jessica's spirits rose. She sat down again on the bench, and watched Randy. Yes, it was definitely going to be Randy. She leaned back and, for the first time in a couple of weeks, felt hopeful. Randy was the nicest kid in the class, and Wendy was certain to be impressed. Her plan was going to work. She smiled thinking about how curious Wendy had been. It was true that she, Jessica, had messed things up somewhat, but tomorrow was another day. And each day Wendy would grow more and more curious. One thing for sure, no day would ever seem as horrible as yesterday.

Yesterday!

Chapter Two

Y esterday, she had dragged herself home from school, stopping at last, unhappily, in front of her own house. It was the prettiest house on the street—pale brown shingles with clumps of red-pink begonia and powdery green dusty miller plants. Jessica climbed heavily up the stairs, brushing against the boxes of fern and marigold that bordered it. She fished her key out of her pocket and opened the antique wooden door.

"Jessica, is that you?"

"Uh huh."

Jessica laid her books down on the Victorian hall stand, and caught a glimpse of her face in the mirror. The light in the hall was golden against the dark wood but the color of her face was green. Not green perhaps—she didn't *look* that much different. Her hair and eyes were still brown, her skin tan, and her teeth white with silver bands. On most days, the golden hall light burnished her edges. She loved to look at herself in that mirror, particularly late in the afternoon when the sunlight caught the reds and yellows of the stained-glass circle in the door. If she stood properly inside its light, she could wear a golden crown of rubies on her head. Rose Red! And

Wendy, with her long blond hair, always liked to be Snow White.

But today the light seemed green.

"I'll be right down, Jess. I'm putting away the laundry. Is that Wendy with you?"

"No."

The pain exploded right under her chest! Jessica began to move quickly. It was a deep, heavy pain, and she needed to set it down somewhere—anywhere. She hurried into the kitchen, and stood sniffing the good baking smells that rose out of the oven. When they first moved to this house five years ago the kitchen had been a small dark room with one side window looking out into an alley. Gradually, the kitchen, like the rest of the house had grown up bright and cheerful. A narrow hall, originally leading out to a back staircase, had been coaxed into more importance. The small kitchen had absorbed it along with a dark, rickety pantry. Now the kitchen was large and bright with sunshine. A pair of sliding doors at the back opened out onto a deck. From where Jessica stood, she could see pots of geranium and lobelia above the green of the garden below. The kitchen had been painted white and gold. In spite of her pain, Jessica noted that Mom had tacked up three patches of wallpaper over the breakfast nook. She tried to focus on them, on the smells from the oven, on anything outside of herself.

"Jessie?"

There was Mom. Jessica tried to struggle against

the trouble inside of her, tried to keep it down and below her throat. Mom's face was puzzled. Jessica started talking.

"Oh, hi, Mom. Which one are you going to take?"

"Which one what?"

"Of the wallpapers. Did you decide yet? They're all kind of nice."

"Oh!" Mom was still looking at her, around her, so she kept talking.

"Maybe that one in the center. I like the blue with the little yellow circles—but maybe this one, with the orange and gold. I like that one too. Maybe that would be better. What do you think, Mom?"

Her mother's face snapped into a smile. "Yes, I do like that one better than the blue. It goes with the curtains, and it's not so overpowering. I'd like to hang up that drawing of the bridge you did in the second grade, and maybe one of Helen's portraits, and that funny pair of cats Arabella painted when she was four. So right now, I think . . ."

Jessica stood there, nodding and pretending to look interested, a little polite smile on her face. When her mother stopped talking, they both looked at each other, and then away embarrassed by the silence. Jessica was thinking desperately of what to say next when her mother said gently, "I made some peanut butter cookies. I thought Wendy was coming over."

There—it was out! And, of course, Jessica knew Mom was bound to find out. But something inside her, in the midst of the pain, struggled to hold on.

She didn't say anything, so Mom asked, "Couldn't she come?"

What was the use? It was more than she could bear anyway. The polite smile vanished, and her true underneath face was revealed.

"She could come—if she wanted."

"Well, I thought . . ." Mom was studying her face with so much loving care. How could anybody hold out against that?

"She doesn't want to come. She says she never wants to come. She says she's not my friend any more."

"But why?" Mom was moving in closer now, but still they hadn't touched. It was only a matter of time before Jessica's tears started flowing, and it was all she could do to gasp out, "It's Barbara!" before her mother reached her and enveloped her in her arms. So she was crying finally, as she knew she would for all those long unhappy days. It felt better, easier and much, much lighter as all the backwash of her growing humiliation and loss exploded out of her.

"Oh Jessie dear! Jessie!"

"She really hates me. I don't know why. I never did anything. All of a sudden, she hates me. She's with Barbara all the time. They eat lunch together, and they play two square, and they . . . they . . . oh, Mom, I wish I was dead."

"No, sweetie, no, don't talk like that. It'll be all right. You'll see. Don't cry like that. Don't, darling!

Come here, sit down next to me. That's right. That's right."

They dropped, enmeshed in each other, down into the window seat. For a while, she wept on her mother's shoulder while her mother patted her back and made soothing sounds above her head. It did feel better leaning there, held in those familiar arms, smelling her mother's warm, mother smell. There had never been any hurt like this one, none that she could remember at least, but there had been other older, ancient hurts, rows and rows of them like dominoes, and all of them collapsing here finally on her mother's shoulder.

"I knew something was wrong when Wendy didn't come by this weekend. I can't remember a weekend when she hasn't been practically living here."

"She and Barbara went ice skating. Barbara slept over Saturday night and they went skating."

"Well, you could have gone too."

"But, Mom," Jessica's voice became a howl, "they didn't ask me. I would have gone even though I hate Barbara. She thinks she's so cool. I hate her! I hate her! Wendy was never like this before. We've been friends since we moved here. We never fought ever until . . ."

Mom smiled, and smoothed Jessica's hair. "Oh, now, you've had plenty of arguments before. Remember when you didn't talk to each other for a couple of weeks, and that summer when Karen came out to visit? Wendy wanted her all to herself and you were jealous? You should know by now the way Wendy is—she's always going through some stage or another. Even Gloria says she can't keep up with her moods." Gloria was Wendy's mother and a friend of Mom's.

"It's different now, Mom. You don't understand."

"Well now, how many times have I heard that before?" Mom said with such a wonderful, confident smile that suddenly Jessica felt comforted. Yes, yes, something inside began singing, it isn't different from other times. Mom's right.

Why hadn't she come right to Mom this time as she always had in the past? Why had she waited? Maybe if she had told Mom right away, this tortured, horrible week never would have happened. Maybe Mom would have patched it up right away, and she and Wendy might be sitting here together this very minute, giggling and eating peanut butter cookies.

"Now you remember," Mom said playfully, "what we used to do when the two of you hated each other and would never ever talk to each other again as long as you both lived?" Mom laughed out loud, and then Jessica was laughing too. She buried her face in Mom's shoulder, nuzzling her and feeling happy and embarrassed.

Mom didn't wait for an answer. "Do you remember? We used to go to Bill's for hamburgers—you and Wendy and Gloria and I."

"I remember," Jessica said happily.

"Well, I haven't seen Gloria in ages. I've been busy with the book, and she's up to her ears in classes. It will be fun all around. I'll call her."

"Oh, do it, Mom, right now. Call her now." Jessica began pushing her mother toward the phone. Mom looked up at the sunflower clock over the refrigerator, and said, "She won't be home until four-thirty or so. I'll phone her then. Should we make it for Saturday?"

"Sure, Mom."

"And don't worry." Mom took her face between both hands and looked deep inside her eyes. But there were no more dark, unhappy corners so Mom kissed her nose, and the two of them sat down at the round oak table and ate warm peanut butter cookies and milk.

"How was school?" Mom asked.

"Okay, Mr. Prince liked my story."

"I knew he would. Did he read it to the class?"

"No, but he hung it up."

"How was the math test?"

"A piece of cake! I think I got an A. Mom, did you put orange rind in the cookies?"

"Yes. How do you like it?"

"Mmm. But I think I like it best with just a nut flavor. Anyway, how's the book going?"

"Just sixteen more recipes to go. Tonight I'm going to try out a Louisiana Gumbo on you all, and don't say you like it if you don't."

"I won't, but I like everything you make."

"Oh you! You'd eat anything—even dog food," Mom said lovingly. They grinned at each other and Jessica felt a warm, comfortable feeling spreading inside of her.

Most of the kids she knew, even Wendy, complained about their mothers. She never did. Mom complained about *her* a lot—that she was sloppy, that she was lazy, that she talked too much, and underneath all the complaining, Jessica knew that she was Mom's favorite. Mom hardly ever complained about Helen, but she and Helen argued almost all the time. Mom spoke only in praises about Arabella, but now that Arabella was away at U. C. Berkeley, she hardly ever came home weekends except when Mom called and asked her to come. Jessica could not believe that a time would come when she would want to leave home.

Jessica loved being with Mom. Anytime she and Wendy weren't playing, she'd stay home and talk to Mom or work with Mom or just be around where she could see her and hear her. Mom always had time for her—always would stop what she was doing to talk and to listen—always was interested in everything Jessica did or thought or wanted. Mom was interested in the games Jessica played, in the work she did in school, and in the kids in her class. Mom was particularly interested in the smart kids, in the ones who were as smart as Jessica, and most of all, in the ones who were maybe a little bit smarter.

All the ups and downs of her friendship with Wendy she had revealed to Mom. Mom had listened, sympathized, and advised. She had never had any secrets from Mom.

"What's that?" Jessica pointed to one of the counters.

"Okra. I had some time finding it fresh." Mom stood up, walked over to her desk, and looked over some papers lying there. She was writing another cookbook. Last year, much to everyone's surprise, her first book, *Soupson,* had been published and had already sold over twenty thousand copies. This second one, on regional American cooking, was called *Of Thee I Sing Cookbook* and Mom had invited all the parents in Jessica's school to contribute recipes. She hoped to include a little personal and regional history along with each recipe selected.

Jessica left her mother comparing three gumbo recipes, and went upstairs to her room. Such a lovely room! Every time she stood in the doorway and looked inside, she marveled at it and at herself for having it.

When they first bought the house, Mom had redone the master bedroom for Dad and herself in pale beige and blue colors. The floor were stained dark with one deep crimson Persian rug in the center. Next, Mom said, it was Arabella's turn. She was thirteen then, in junior high school, and she had seniority, being the oldest child. Arabella's room finally was done in soft pink and lavender tones. Her floor was also stained dark with a round deep-rose rug with red tassels. Helen came next. She was not at all interested in her room, and kept saying she didn't have time. But Mom wanted Helen to enjoy her room, and she kept after her. Finally, Helen's room was finished too, and just as lovely as the others. Helen, sixteen now and a student at George Washington High School, had always been the "politico" in the family, as Dad said. Right now she was president of the student council, but even when she was younger she had always been something in something. Her room turned out to be more modern than the others in golds and browns and oranges. Posters of different political campaigns Mom sent away for hung on her walls. The floors of her bedroom were also stained dark with an interesting orange and gold Danish rug.

Then, a year ago, it was finally Jessica's turn.

"You can do your own room any way you like," Mom told her. And Jessica was ready. "I want bright blue wall-to-wall carpets, and light blue walls. I want to paint my furniture red, white, and blue, and I want a striped red and white bedspread with bright red sheets and pillows. I don't want any curtains, but I do want a dark blue shade with white stars."

Jessica knew that her mother would be pleased. She was the only one of the children who knew exactly what she wanted. Mom had been amazed and delighted. "You really have done your homework and I am proud of you. You know I want each of you girls to have exactly the kind of room you want."

Then they got down to shopping. In Dad's store,

Mom showed her a wonderful off-white, soft, shaggy flokati rug from Greece.

"Oh, it's marvelous, Mom, just marvelous, but I want wall-to-wall blue carpeting."

Mom said she could have anything she wanted, but she did point out that wall-to-wall carpeting was sort of old-fashioned and unoriginal. Of course it was entirely up to her, Mom said, but Jessica finally decided on dark stained floors with the wonderful, shaggy, off-white flokati rug in the center. Mom showed her so many different kinds of rooms of furniture, and so many pictures in magazines and so many beautiful, wonderful fabrics that somewhere along the line, she realized that the red, white, and blue room was really tacky. With Mom's help her room now was a beautiful cool, glowing room full of soft greens and whites and blues. It was the kind of room you almost wanted to tiptoe in. Of all the rooms, Jessica thought hers the loveliest.

She meant to be neat and tidy but often she threw her books around and forgot to make her bed in the morning. Mom complained but she always made Jessica's bed, and straightened up so that every afternoon when Jessica came home from school and stood in the doorway of her room, it was like looking into a strange and beautiful land that mistakenly belonged to her.

Now she took a book, sat down in her white rocker, and tried to read. But her thoughts kept straying. She kept watching the clock, and at four-thirty went flying downstairs to the kitchen.

"Go on, Mom, call Gloria. You still haven't."

"Oh, that's right," said Mom. "Wait until I comb my hair."

"But, Mom, you're only talking on the phone."

"I know, but there now. I'm ready." Mom removed her apron, tucked her blouse into her skirt, and picked up the phone.

Jessica sat down on a kitchen chair opposite to her mother's desk in the kitchen, and waited.

"Hello, Gloria?" said her mother, smiling into the phone. "It's Sonja."

"I know . . . ages . . . How's everything? . . . Oh, really! . . . Hmm . . . That's great . . . Keep it up . . . He's fine . . . Yes . . . Arabella? You know when they're first out of the nest they forget they have a home . . . Helen? . . . busy, busy, busy . . . She never has a free moment to talk . . . I know, and I am but sometimes I wish she had a few more ordinary interests . . . Jessica? . . . Fine, and that's really why I'm calling . . . Yes, you've been hearing too (laughter) . . . I know, like old times . . . So, I guess it's time for lunch at Bill's . . . How about Saturday? . . . Yes, it has been ages . . . Sure, ask her. I'll hold on."

Mom smiled and nodded to Jessica. She put her hand over the mouthpiece of the phone and whispered very softly with exaggerated mouth movements, "She's going to ask Wendy."

"Yes. Hello (laughter) . . . Oh? (Mom's smile started fading) . . . She did? . . . Well, I just can't . . . Oh, Gloria, don't get so worked up. You know kids and their moods . . . Maybe I should talk to her. Why don't you just tell her that Sonja wants to talk to her . . ."

Mom gave Jessica a comforting nod, but again Jessica felt the pain swelling inside her. This time it *was* different. She'd known it was different all along.

"Hello, Gloria? . . . She really won't . . . Well, isn't she being, uh, determined . . . Oh, Gloria, don't make such a fuss . . . if she won't, she won't . . . It'll blow over. It always does . . . You know the way she is . . . Oh! . . . Oh! . . . No! . . . Gloria, don't tell her *that!* Let's just give it a little time. I'll call you next week or so . . . Fine . . . Don't feel so bad! . . . It's not your fault . . . That's right . . . And my best to Frank."

Jessica was crying even before her mother hung up. "See! See!" she yelled, "I told you it was different this time."

"Poor Gloria," Mom said, "she's so upset. She's really a lovely person but she just can't handle that child."

"But, Mom," Jessica wailed, "you promised you'd fix it. You promised."

"Oh, I will," her mother said, shaking her head, "but I must say I think Wendy is the most self-centered kid I know. Maybe you remember I once told you that I thought Wendy was selfish, and that I didn't like the way you always had to cater to her."

Jessica was crying hard now. "But you were the one who told me to make friends with her. You always wanted me to play with her. You always said

23

she was so smart, and had such a nice family, and now she hates me. Oh, I wish I was dead!"

Mom pulled her into her lap, and told her not to worry, it was going to work out just fine. Mom said to give it a little time, and maybe in a week or so she could have a slumber party, and invite a few girls, including Wendy. Mom said the best thing was for Jessica to stop thinking about it, and not to worry.

Not to worry! That night in bed, Jessica tried different ways of curling up and twisting away from the worry. But it was always there. She couldn't escape it. Finally, she flopped over on her back, straightened out, looked up at the ceiling, and worried.

Why had it all started, and what could she do to get Wendy back?

She couldn't really answer the why. They hadn't argued. As a matter of fact, Wendy had been mad at Susie Edelstein for a couple of days before. Susie was kind of funny-looking, and had a big nose, so Wendy kept calling, "Oh, Susie Frankenstein—I mean Edelstein." Jessica couldn't help laughing when Wendy said it, but she did think it was mean. Wendy said she had it coming because Susie started the whole thing by calling her the Easter Bunny.

"Oh, she was only kidding because you always have egg salad for lunch."

"So she always has a big nose, and looks more like a Frankenstein than an Edelstein."

It *was* funny watching Susie trying to act casual. After a while, the other kids began calling her Frankenstein too.

Anyway, *they* hadn't argued. Wendy hadn't been mad at *her*. They were even planning to make matching towel tote bags later that week.

Suddenly everything was Barbara. But why and how? One day she and Wendy were best friends, and the next day they were not. Why? She tried to remember if there had been any glances or laughter or remarks on her part that Wendy could have misinterpreted. There were none. There seldom were.

What could she do to make up with Wendy? That was the important question. She had to do something because it was a lonely, dreary world without her. Wendy always had something exciting to talk about, always had a fun scheme planned. Every morning Jessica woke up looking forward to the day because Wendy was there. It was impossible to think of life without Wendy. What would she do? What would she think about? What would she say?

She felt the tears beginning to flood her eyes. No, not yet. There had to be *something* she could do. But what? This time, Mom wasn't going to be any help. She would have to figure out something all by herself. Jessica lay on her back a long, long time that night, thinking.

Chapter Three

Tthat was yesterday. She had stayed awake for hours and then, somewhere between sleep and waking, the plan was born. Early in the morning, with her door locked, she had written the first note, and dropped it on her seat as the class left for gym.

Wendy had been curious. She would continue to be curious—very, very curious. She would want to see each note, would wonder who had sent them, and, Jessica hoped, would grow jealous. It would make her realize that somebody else in the class liked Jessica too. Maybe she would worry. Most likely she would just decide to make up, and one day in the future, Jessica could tell her the truth and they would both laugh over it.

Maybe today she, Jessica, had been a bit overanxious. Tomorrow would be better. She rocked back and forth thoughtfully on the bench and reached up to touch her locket. It wasn't there. Nervously she thought—well, if she can give hers away, I can throw mine away. We'll get new lockets after we make up.

But the nervousness grew stronger and stronger as the day passed. She kept waking up at night, reaching for the locket and touching nothing. In the morning she was desperate.

"Where are you going so early?" Mom asked. "It's only seven-twenty. You've got nearly another hour."

She stood there on the stairs in her blue bathrobe, and looked down at Jessica, fully dressed and putting on her jacket.

"I . . . I've got to meet someone."

"Oh? Wendy? Did you call her yesterday?"

"No, Mom, somebody else."

Mom started down the steps. "Who?"

"Somebody else—but, Mom, I've got to go."

Mom was all the way down the stairs now. "You haven't eaten breakfast, Jessica. Just let me make you some toast and eggs."

"Mom, I had some Life and—please—I'm late."

Mom began smiling. "It must be someone kind of special. What's her name?"

Desperately, Jessica threw out the first name that came to mind. "It's Rachel."

"Rachel Ross?"

"Uh huh."

"Oh that's nice. She's such a smart girl, such a big reader. I always thought you both had a lot in common."

"I know, Mom, you always told me so. But I have to go now."

"If you wait a minute, I'll drive you. It's so early nobody else is out."

"I can't wait, Mom, and there are plenty of people out. See you later."

"Jessica!"

She was nearly out the door when she heard her

mother's voice, urgent, hurt. She hurried back. "Sorry, Mom, I'm in such a hurry, I nearly forgot."

Her mother's blue eyes were large and clear and she could see herself in both of them. Jessica tried to make her kiss seem extra loving. Suddenly, she felt guilty and sorry for her mother but she didn't know why. Mom pulled her over, kissed her hungrily, and said, "Well, have a good day, and be careful when you cross the street."

"Mom!" She hurried out the door, ran nearly all the way, and was out of breath by the time she reached the schoolyard. Nobody else was around, and she raced over to the garbage can and looked inside. It was empty, and she burst into a loud wail.

"I've got to find it! I've got to find it!" she said out loud, clenching her fists. She hurried across the yard, the tears rolling down her face. "Mr. Feeney, Mr. Feeney!" she yelled.

The custodian was in the cafeteria, opening a large cardboard box, when she finally tracked him down.

"Oh, Mr. Feeney," she sobbed, "what happened to all the garbage from yesterday? I've got to find the garbage. Where is it?"

"Well," said Mr. Feeney pleasantly, "most of it must be out swimming in the bay by now." He studied Jessica's desolate face. "Why are you so interested in the garbage?"

"I lost something very valuable. Oh, what can I do?"

"What did you lose?"

"A locket, Mr. Feeney, a gold one with my initials,

J.F., on the back, and I'll die if I don't find it and—
oh—that's it, that's it. You found it, Mr. Feeney, oh
thanks, Mr. Feeney."

"I found it wrapped around a carrot stick, and
figured somebody would be looking for it." Mr.
Feeney had taken the locket out of his pocket and
was holding it up. Her locket, her wonderful precious
locket. It felt so good around her neck. She swore to
herself that she'd never take it off again. Never!
Never! Not even when she was showering or swimming. Never!

She felt happy and comfortable, and the good feelings lasted until she saw that Barbara was back in
school again, wearing the poison locket. Barbara and
Wendy were all wrapped up in each other, giggling
and whispering in their own exclusive magic circle.
Wendy never looked at her once until library period.

Carefully she placed the note on top of her books.
When she came back to the table, after the bell
rang, there it was, with J.F. clearly written, but this
time, the handwriting was wavy—very different from
yesterday's note. Jessica was pleased with it. She
picked it up eagerly, opened it, and read

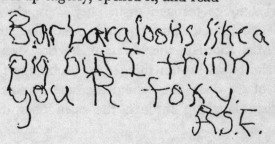

Jessica couldn't help laughing out loud. Then, guiltily, she looked around. A few of the kids were watching her, including Wendy and Barbara.

Was she really foxy? She couldn't wait to get into the girls' room, and look at herself in the mirror. A.S.F. was certainly right about Barbara though. She not only looked like a pig—she was a pig. Jessica glared at Barbara with hate, trying to catch her eye. Barbara began looking all around the library—everywhere except back at Jessica.

"What does the weirdo have to say today?" Wendy asked. Jessica knew that Wendy was dying to read the note. No matter how cool she looked, Wendy was curious. Wendy was always curious.

"You wouldn't be interested," Jessica said, slowly folding up the note.

"I bet I know who it's from." Wendy stood there grinning at her, showing lots of teeth.

"Come on, let's go, Wendy," Barbara said, tugging at her arm.

Jessica's eyes moved away from them, and followed Randy as the class started filing out of the library. He and Jeff Choy arrived at the door at the same time, and began jostling each other as they both tried to go through first. They were clowning now, laughing and pushing and pretending to be angry. Miss Riordan, the librarian, hurried over but before she could say anything they broke apart and fell out of the door, one behind the other. You could hear them laughing through the open door. Some friends made each other feel good. Some friends didn't tease or show their teeth or make fun of you.

Wendy snickered. "I bet it's from Freddie Arnold. He's just your type, isn't he, and the initials are just right, only backward. I bet his middle name starts with an S."

Freddie Arnold wasn't even in their grade. He was only a fourth-grader, and the freakiest kid in the school. He always had hives and was scratching himself and making trouble. He couldn't sit still, and nobody could stand him.

Don't let her bother you, Jessica told herself. Think about Randy and Jeff and being foxy. In an icy voice, she said, "Wendy, I'd like to talk to you for a minute—alone."

"I'll wait for you outside." Barbara picked up her books and moved toward the door.

"No, wait! I'm coming too," Wendy said quickly.

"Wendy," Jessica insisted, "hold on just a second! It won't take long."

They were alone together in the library. Miss Riordan said, "Go along, girls, there's another class waiting."

"Well?" said Wendy.

"Wendy," Jessica began, trying to be cool. She could see Wendy straining to go, struggling to be free of her. The old fear and desperation was too much, and the words broke out of her. "Why are you like this? What did I do? Whatever it is, I'm sorry. Please, let's be friends again. Please, Wendy!"

Wendy's face looked like she was going to cry. "You make me sick," she said. "Leave me alone! Leave me alone!" Then she grabbed her books and ran out the door. Jessica sat down, licked her braces, said to herself, "I'm not going to cry," and felt the tears beginning to flow. So she took a deep breath, reached up behind her neck, took off the locket and threw it out in the wastebasket near Miss Riordan's desk. That felt better, and she hurried out of the library as the next class started coming in.

A couple of minutes later, she came charging back. She fished her locket out of the basket and left before anybody noticed.

Back in her classroom, the kids were busy working on the underwater collage. Wendy and Barbara were holding cutouts of underwater plants up against different parts of the collage. Randy was bending over his desk, working on a drawing. He kept his head down, eyes stubbornly fastened on his drawing. Well, of course, he wouldn't be looking at her. Out of the corner of her eye she noticed that Wendy had seen her come through the door and had whispered something in Barbara's ear. Well, she wasn't just going to stand there and let them make fun of her.

She began moving toward the reading corner, and as she passed behind Randy's desk she stopped casually and looked down over his shoulder.

"Oh!" she couldn't help saying.

Randy looked up. Then he put his hands over his paper, and said, "Don't look!"

"Oh!" Jessica repeated.

Randy kept his hands over his work, wrinkled his face and said, "It's terrible, isn't it?"

"Well," Jessica said carefully, "you're not through yet so . . ."

"I just can't do it," he said helplessly. He took his hands off the paper, picked up a marking pen, and made a big cross over his drawing. It was of a blue shark but the nose was too sharp and the body looked fat and pregnant.

"Well . . ." said Jessica, wishing she could think of something else to say.

"Maybe I just ought to make a snail," Randy said unhappily. "I guess I could do that."

Mr. Prince had said that everyone in the class had to work on the underwater collage so that when parents came for open house and wanted to see something hanging up done by their child, he could at least point to the collage. Jessica never had to worry about her things hanging up. On any given day she was sure to have a story or a drawing or even a math paper.

The underwater collage was filled with Jessica's drawings—a pair of battling sting rays, several pink anemones of different sizes, one large, blue-eyed octopus, and two sea horses. She had also drawn three exquisite starfish, but Mr. Prince said better let the kids who couldn't draw, do the starfish.

"Maybe you could do a starfish," she suggested.

"Thanks a lot," Randy looked away, hurt.

"Oh, but I didn't mean . . ." Her big mouth! Why did she have to go and say starfish? Why couldn't she just have shut up and looked sympathetic?

"It's all right," Randy said, looking at her and smiling again. "Everybody can't draw like *you*."

The day was going to be a winner, after all. Somebody was looking at her, somebody besides Randy. It was Wendy, eyes narrowed, forehead creased.

"Thanks," she said softly, and moved away. She wasn't going to let Wendy spoil this. She'd had enough of Wendy and her teeth.

There were other people in the world besides Wendy. Hadn't Randy Jackson said, "Everybody can't draw like you." What a nice boy he was! She could see herself with him and Jeff Choy, horsing around, pushing and tussling at the library door.

It had not been part of her plan to make a new friend—but why not? Wendy wouldn't mind, or would she? She felt a stab of guilt, thinking about Wendy. Wendy would always be her best friend, but maybe Wendy wouldn't want her to be friends with Randy Jackson. Maybe Wendy would be jealous. What then? She touched her locket and looked over at Wendy. Wendy had an arm around Barbara's shoulder. Jessica heaved a sigh of relief. Wendy wasn't jealous. As a matter of fact, Wendy didn't seem to care at all. Now that wasn't good either. Wendy hadn't even asked to see the new note. Randy Jackson was becoming too much of a distraction, which was not part of her plan. Wendy was supposed to have seen this note, and questioned her again about A.S.F., and then she was supposed to imply that it was somebody interesting like Randy.

Well, tomorrow she would make sure that Wendy saw the note. She would put it where Wendy couldn't help but see it.

Chapter Four

W ell, did you meet Rachel in time?" Mom
was waiting for her when she got home from
school that day.

"Uh huh—oh, Mom, there's a rip in my jacket."

"Here let me have it," Mom said. "It's just in the
seam. Do you want a brownie with your milk?"

"Sure."

"Come on in the kitchen. I'll stop and have a cup
of tea with you."

The kitchen was fragrant with brownie smells.
Mom took four or five brownies out of a baking pan,
arranged them on a blue-willow plate, poured a glass
of milk for Jessica in an amber-colored glass, and sat
down with her at the round oak table.

"Aren't you having tea?"

"Oh, that's right." Mom put up the kettle, then
sat down again, and watched Jessica eat her brownie.

"Where does Rachel live?"

"I don't know. Mom, what's for dinner tonight?"

"Oh, just a typical midwestern meal. I'm a little
tired today. Steak, corn, salad, and brownies. Nothing for the cookbook."

"Mmm. I don't mind steak," Jessica said kindly. She took another brownie, and her mother watched as she chewed and licked at some stray crumbs that caught in her braces.

"I always liked Rachel. She seems so good-natured for such a smart girl."

"Yes, Mom."

"It's a good idea for you to have other friends besides Wendy—especially somebody like Rachel."

"Yes, Mom."

"Oh, and by the way, I called Gloria this morning —just to say hello—and . . ."

Jessica's legs began trembling. "Did she say anything? I mean about me?"

"Well—she's been trying to talk to Wendy but . . ." Mom made a face. "She really has her hands full with that child. Such a spoiled brat! Honestly, sometimes I think you'd be better off without her for a friend."

"But, Mom, what did she say? Why is Wendy mad at me?"

"We had a long talk, and I suggested she might want to take Wendy for counseling. It sounds to me like that girl is going to need some help in straightening out."

"Please, Mom, what did she say?"

"I think she's just jealous of you."

"Wendy? Jealous of me?"

"Yes. She says, believe it or not, that you're a mama's baby." Mom looked very annoyed. "Imagine saying a thing like that. You're so independent and original. You walked earlier than either of the other girls, and you always did more things on your own. I've always gone out of my way to be nice to Wendy, but if she . . ."

"What else, Mom, what else did she say?"

"Well, she also felt you were turning her mother against her—which is just stupid. Naturally her mother is going to correct her if she's wrong, and she's usually wrong where you're concerned. She says you always make her look bad, and you always come out the good one. Something about Mr. Prince yelling at her, and not you a week or so ago."

"Mr. Prince?"

"I don't remember exactly. Probably you weren't even involved, but she said she always gets the blame and usually you're just as guilty."

"Mr. Prince?" Dimly, Jessica remembered something, some small isolated island in her memory. It was a fire drill. She and Wendy were talking and Mr. Prince put his hand on Wendy's shoulder and told her to stop. Just that? Was that it?

". . . so I told Gloria to tell Wendy that if she keeps up this way, she won't have any friends at all. Maybe I'll try to talk to her myself."

Mom's pretty face was rosy with indignation. Jessica felt a rising current of irritation. "Please, Mom, don't talk to Wendy. It's going to work out. I'm sure of that. Please don't say anything to Wendy."

"Of course I won't if you don't want me to, but

believe me, I'm tempted. Anyway, Gloria did say that Barbara was really quite a nice little girl and that she even reminded her of you."

"Of me!" Now it was Jessica's turn to be indignant.

"Yes, you. She said Barbara was a sweet, polite child who smiled a lot—like you, and . . ."

"I don't smile a lot."

"Yes, you do, and you are sweet and polite and smart and good and kind and Mama's darling girl and . . ."

So there they were cuddling again, which wasn't exactly unpleasant, but Jessica had her mind on other things.

Next day, the note fell out of her folder on her way back from gym. Barbara and Wendy were right behind her. She planned that Wendy would pick it up and read it quickly before handing it over. But Wendy just pushed right into her, causing her to bump Linda Hall.

"I'm sorry," she said to Linda. Then she had to bend down and pick up the note herself.

"That's okay." Linda glanced down at the note in her hand. "You sure have been getting a lot of notes lately."

"Well . . ." Jessica looked down at the folded note in her hand. This time the J.F. had been cut out of a magazine and pasted on.

"Can I see it?"

"I don't know what it says. It might be personal."

"Open it up and see."

Linda had good manners, and she looked in another direction while Jessica opened the note, and read

Will You MEET ME TOMORROW at the public library AFTER SCHOOL ? I think YOU R cool

AS F

"Well," said Linda, "what does it say?"

Jessica looked away embarrassed. "I wish I could tell you, Linda, I really do. But I guess I shouldn't say. It's supposed to be a secret."

Out of the corner of her eye, she could see Wendy now looking at her. She knew that Wendy must be dying to see the note, so she said a little louder, "I'm not supposed to show it to *anybody*."

"Who is it from?"

"Well, the person doesn't say. It's signed A.S.F., and I figure that means A Secret Friend."

"That's neat," Linda said smiling. "I wish I had a secret friend."

"Hey, Jessica," Wendy yelled, "what did Freddie Arnold have to say today?"

Jessica concentrated on Linda. "I really wish I could show it to *you*."

There was the sound of laughter from Wendy's direction. Linda was acting as if she hadn't heard Wendy and was trying hard not to smile. "That's okay," she said kindly. "Lucky you!"

"Lucky me!" Jessica held onto that during the rest of the day. Wendy had to read that note. She just had to. But no opportunity presented itself. Wendy kept stubbornly away from her.

Randy Jackson smiled at her during math. He was wearing a pair of shades today—those mirrored sunglasses where the wearer can look at you without you knowing that he was. Was he looking at her? Was he thinking, That's a nice, friendly girl. She smiles a lot because she's good and kind. Maybe she would like to be friends with me. Maybe I should try to get together with her after school.

There was a book about horses on his desk, and Jessica lingered there on her way back from sharpening her pencil.

"Do you like horse stories?" she asked.

Randy shrugged. "I like dog stories better, but Mr. Prince said this was a good one."

"I like dog stories too," she lied. "They've got a lot over at the public library in my neighborhood. That's the Anza branch—over on Anza and Thirty-seventh. Where do you go?"

"To Western Addition. I live a couple of blocks away."

Carefully Jessica told him, "I'll be going to the library tomorrow afternoon. I always go on Fridays."

Randy nodded and smiled. She couldn't see his

eyes since they were hidden behind the shades. But she could see Wendy's eyes—directed at her and Randy. She dropped her voice and said softly, "That's the Anza Branch I go to—on Anza and Thirty-seventh. They have lots of good dog stories. I'll probably get there around four and spend an hour or so. There's always so many books to look at."

"I guess you're a pretty big reader," Randy said.

"Oh yes, I am—not like Rachel Ross though."

"Nobody reads as much as Rachel Ross," Randy agreed, and they both laughed. She stood there a second or two, and then there really was nothing else to say, so she returned to her seat.

That felt good—talking and laughing with Randy. Would he pick up on her hint? Would he come to the library tomorrow? What if he did? They'd meet in front and walk up the stone steps together. He'd say, "Now where's those dog stories you promised?" And she could introduce him to Miss Chandler, the librarian. She could say, "Miss Chandler, this is my friend Randy Jackson. He likes dog stories."

She daydreamed for a while and then remembered that Wendy still hadn't seen the note. Wendy *had* to see the note, especially now since it looked as if Randy would be coming. She left it opened on her desk, and sure enough, while she was off in the math corner, she spotted Wendy furtively reading it. Good! Now her plan was really working out and Wendy knew she would be at the library tomorrow.

Wendy was waiting for her in the yard after

school. Her heart began pounding in her ears. Was Wendy ready to make up? And what should she say about Randy? She flashed her friendliest smile at Wendy.

"I left something at your house," Wendy said coldly, "and I want it back."

"Sure Wendy, come on over now and you can pick it up. What is it?"

"My blue sweater. You also have my eyebrow pencil, and my Love's Fresh Lemon Body Mist. I want them all back."

"But I paid for the eyebrow pencil, and we both chipped in for the body mist."

"You can keep the eyebrow pencil if you're going to be cheap, but I want my sweater back, and I paid for the Lemon Body Mist. I remember."

"Okay, Wendy, whatever you say. You can have the eyebrow pencil too. Let's go."

"I'm not going home with you—ever. You can bring in the sweater and the other stuff tomorrow. And also, you can tell your mother to stop bugging me."

"Listen, Wendy, I think I know why you're mad, and you're right. Mr. Prince was wrong. I was talking too, and I'm sorry he was wrong. Do you want me to say something to him?"

Wendy's voice was icy. "I don't know what you're talking about. Just get out of my way—and bring those things in tomorrow."

Jessica sat down on the bench and surveyed

Wendy's back growing smaller and smaller. She could feel the tears brimming over in her eyes, and had a sudden longing to be home in Mom's arms, her head on Mom's shoulder. Maybe she could tell Mom about the notes and Mom could suggest what Jessica should do next.

But then, the notes would no longer be her secret if she told Mom. It was the first time she had a secret that neither Mom nor Wendy knew about. She felt suddenly proud of her independence and miserably lonely.

Desperately, she looked around the schoolyard. Over in one corner in the sunshine sat a familiar figure arched over a book in her lap. It was Rachel Ross, and she raised her eyes without changing her position as Jessica approached.

"Hi, Rachel!" Jessica said humbly. Everybody in the class, including Mr. Prince, was awed by the amount of time Rachel spent reading. Sometimes Jessica wondered why, with all that reading inside her, Rachel wasn't a more spectacular student. She had a slow, languorous way of speaking and often seemed surprised when she was called upon to answer questions in class. Everyone assumed that her intelligence was so far beyond anyone else's that she simply could not be bothered doing the ordinary, everyday classwork that everyone else did.

"Hello!" Rachel returned in a deep, slow voice, and went back to her book.

"What are you reading?" Jessica sat down next to her.

Languidly, Rachel moved her eyes sideways without shifting her position.

"It's called," she said slowly, *"Big Tiger and Christian."*

"What a big book!" said Jessica. "Is it good?"

Rachel shrugged, and turned her eyes downward again.

"I read a marvelous book a few days ago called *Nilda.* It's about a girl who grows up in . . ."

"I read it," said Rachel, eyes still down.

"Oh! What did you think of it?"

Rachel shrugged.

"Did you read a book called *Warrior Scarlet?* I don't usually like historical books, but this one was so sad. It's about a handicapped boy and I cried at the end."

"It was all right," said Rachel slowly. Her eyes moved again toward Jessica, and this time her head turned just a little.

Grateful for the unusual show of interest on Rachel's part, Jessica asked respectfully, "What's your favorite book?"

Rachel slowly straightened up, and appeared to shudder. Her soft eyes blinked.

"I guess it must be hard for you to pick *one* because you read so much. Maybe you have a few you like best."

"I think," Rachel finally said in a low, important voice (Jessica had to bend forward to hear her), "that I like all of them the same."

"The same?" Jessica looked into the soft, expressionless face in wonder. How was it possible to like all books the same? Or all colors? Or all people? Or all foods? Slowly Rachel's head revolved downward, and Jessica watched her thoughtfully. The same? Perhaps this was part of Rachel's superiority. Maybe she said things that seemed very stupid, but were actually on a different, higher plane.

Rachel was engrossed in her book now, and Jessica found herself engrossed in Rachel. Mom was eager for them to be friends, and usually she agreed with Mom's judgment. Mom had liked Wendy and it was Mom who had originally promoted the friendship.

Maybe Mom had been wrong about Wendy. Maybe she was wrong about Rachel too. Even though Rachel might be smart, she was also dull and colorless. She inspected Rachel's pale, limp face, and thought to herself, "I don't want her as a friend no matter what Mom thinks."

Suddenly Rachel looked up and smiled a wan, uncertain smile. It made Jessica feel guilty. "Uh, how's the book?" she asked quickly.

"It's all right," Rachel said slowly.

"Brr! It's getting cold." Jessica stood up. "How come you're reading here instead of inside your house?"

"I have to watch my brother," said Rachel. "My mother told me to stay here after school and watch him while he played."

"Which one is your brother?" asked Jessica, looking into the clumps of assorted boys that dotted the schoolyard.

Slowly, Rachel's head turned, surveying the scene. "He's not here," she said tonelessly. "Maybe he went home." She stood up slowly. "I guess I'd better go too," and she moved heavily off.

"Me too," said Jessica, trying not to look into Rachel's soft, dull face. "Good-by, Rachel." She hurried off, thinking with pity about poor, dull Rachel who had only her books to entertain her. It consoled her for her own disappointing afternoon. After all, she did have tomorrow to look forward to. Thank goodness for A.S.F. and Randy Jackson. She didn't know how she'd ever manage if it wasn't for the notes. Wendy was being so mean. How she hated Wendy.

Jessica reached up, took off her poison locket and knelt at the corner, holding it over the grate of a sewer. She let it dangle from one finger, and thought about Randy. Friends should make you feel good. She let the locket swing from her finger—closer and closer to the grate. This time it would be for good. Once it went down, she would not be able to get it back. A few more swings, and then she stood up, fastened the locket around her neck, and started home.

Chapter Five

J essica came carefully around the corner and looked anxiously at the window of her house. No face watching for her as she had feared. She opened the door carefully.

Inside she could hear Mom's voice on the telephone, high and urgent. "Well, they *wouldn't* stay— said they were going to a chamber concert. She called him Bob, and he seemed in a big hurry to get her away . . . Well, I did, Alex, I did, but she was in such a hurry, she couldn't . . ."

She hurried into the kitchen, sat down, and watched Mom as she spoke to Dad. Mom was combing her hair as she spoke, and cast an anguished look in Jessica's direction.

". . . next weekend . . . God knows where she's going this weekend. She came to get her hiking boots. You know Arabella. The last time she used those boots must have been in the Girl Scouts. I think you should do something . . . *I am not excited* . . . All right, all right . . . I'll wait, but hurry!"

She hung up. Jessica asked, "Was Arabella here? With a man?"

Her mother's eyes opened very wide in fake innocence. "Yes, she was with . . . with Dr. Petersen. He's one of her instructors at Berkeley. I think she said music history."

"Why didn't she stay? I haven't seen her in ages."

"They were going to a chamber music group. Dr. Petersen invited Arabella to hear his friends play. I'm sure it was very nice of him."

"Is he young and cute?"

"Not exactly," said her mother, terror written all over her face. "He must be a man of about thirty-five or thirty-six, and I wouldn't call him cute."

"What do you think Dad should do?"

"Oh, Jessica, stop asking me stupid questions. And where were you so late, by the way?"

"It's not late—not even four o'clock."

Luckily, her mother was too busy worrying about Arabella to spend any time worrying about her. As soon as Dad came home, the two of them closed themselves off in their room and didn't come out for over an hour.

"It's Arabella," Jessica told Helen when she came home. She'd been watching out for Helen, and couldn't wait to tell her. "Mom's all upset because Arabella stopped by with a teacher of hers named Dr. Petersen, and . . ."

"Bob?" Helen said with interest. "Oh, what's he like?"

"I didn't see him. They left before I came home. I don't know anything about him except that he's old, maybe thirty-five or thirty-six."

"Thirty-four," Helen said, sitting down and smiling agreeably into her sister's downcast face, "and divorced with three kids."

Jessica was disappointed. This time, for sure, she thought she had something to tell Helen that she didn't already know, or said she knew.

"But how do you know all that?" she cried.

"Because Arabella told me last time she was in. She said she went to see him one afternoon to ask him a question about Palestrina, ended up having coffee, and then dinner with him, and says he's one of the greatest guys she's ever met."

"You mean you knew all about him for four weeks."

"Uh huh."

"But Mom didn't know."

Helen laughed. "Well, you don't think Arabella was going to tell Mom, do you? You know Mom."

"But you didn't tell Mom either."

"I stopped telling Mom things when I was twelve." She smiled kindly at Jessica—one of those kind smiles that are so mean. "I guess that gives you about a year and a half to go."

"I don't tell Mom everything," Jessica protested.

"Oh no!" Helen mocked. "Tell me one thing you don't tell Mom." She watched Jessica's face while she waited. Then she said, with not quite so mean a smile, "That's all right. I did too, and so did Arabella."

"I don't tell her everything," Jessica said again, "but I'm not going to tell you what I don't tell her."

"You mean like how many times you went to the bathroom."

"No," Jessica yelled, "like today. I did something secret today that nobody knows."

"Sure! Sure!" Helen laughed, and went upstairs to her room.

"Well, I did too," Jessica shrieked up the stairs after her.

"Jessica, please!" Dad said, coming out of his room. "Don't yell like that. Mom has a headache, and it doesn't help if you yell."

"Dad," Jessica said, "what are you going to do?"

"Do?" Dad acted surprised.

"I mean about Arabella and Dr. Petersen."

"Well, Jessica, there's nothing really to do and no reason to be upset. Arabella is eighteen, and has always been sensible and dependable. She's an adult now, and I think we can trust her to choose her own friends."

"But what are you going to do about Dr. Petersen?"

"Nothing," said her father.

Mom was sulky during dinner so Dad tried to keep the conversation going.

"Guess what color carpet we put down today in the new Milady's Department Store?" he asked. Dad had the largest rug store in San Francisco. He had worked it up from the smallest rug store twenty years ago, and made lots of money along the way.

"What?" Jessica asked.

"Bright red," Dad said, looking at Mom for some

reaction. "The designer had all the furnishings painted green too. She told me she worked it all out with a psychologist—a behavior modification planner —who said red and green make people think of Christmas, and Christmas makes people want to spend their money, and Milady's Department Store also wants them to spend their money so . . ."

"Oh, Dad, that's disgusting," Helen said. "How can you go along with that?"

"It wasn't my idea," said Dad. "I just sell them the carpeting, and it's good and expensive, I might add, so you could say that the first victim of this red and green plot is the department store itself. For half of what they're paying they could have bought better, more durable (but less colorful), carpeting."

"How can you bear to be in this business, altogether?" Helen said. "To pander to the worst instincts of greedy, predatory people who are trying to make a fast buck off people who can't afford it?"

"Lots of people can afford it," Dad said mildly. "And besides, I have other customers besides Milady's. Lots of people whose homes are made more beautiful because of my carpets."

"Will you two stop arguing," Mom said in a cranky voice. "I want to know, Alex, when you're going to Berkeley."

"Dad and I are not arguing," Helen argued. "You always say we're arguing when all we're doing is having a discussion. He's an intelligent man, even though he's working at a business that's beneath his abilities, and . . ."

"You are a snob, an idealist, and an intellectual," Dad said lovingly, "and it's a good thing you have a rich father to support your vices. Now, to answer your question, Sonja, I wasn't aware that I was going to Berkeley."

"Is it snobbishness to want to do something to benefit people and not to rob them?"

"I really don't think it's very respectful of you, Helen, to say that your father is robbing anyone," Mom said, "and Alex, you said you had to check over a new medical building in Berkeley that asked for some advice on rugs."

"Oh, that's right. Probably I'll go on Monday in the afternoon. Why?"

"Because," Mom said, "I think I'll go along with you. We can have lunch with Arabella, the two of us, and I can see the exhibit at Kroeber Hall while you're talking to your client."

"Sonja, I told you, I wasn't going to get into this."

"Into what?" Mom's eyes were very wide. "We always said it would be fun to drop in on Arabella and . . ."

"I will not drop in on Arabella," said Dad.

"Of course not, Alex. You're right. I'll call her, and let her know we're coming. Is twelve okay?"

"No, it isn't. I'll be busy at least until twelve."

"Well, we'll make it one then, and what time will you be through later in the afternoon?"

"Not until four-thirty at the earliest."

"Oh, that will give me lots of time to see the exhibit. I understand there's a whole group of American Indian food implements that might be very helpful for me. The only thing is, we won't be home until five-thirty or six, so, Jessica, if you don't want to be alone, I can ask Grandma to come over."

"Oh that's okay, Mom," Jessica said, "I don't mind being alone at all."

Now Dad became sulky and Mom was cheerful.

"Well now, I haven't had a chance to say hello to either one of you two. Helen, how was school?"

"Fine."

"Anything special doing?"

"Nope."

"I don't know, Helen, you always seem to have plenty to say to Dad, but when I ask you anything, the answer is either fine or nope." She smiled, but there was a hurting behind the smile that Jessica felt. Mom turned toward her, and Jessica tried to look encouraging and enthusiastic.

"And how was your day, Jessie?"

Jessica prepared to discuss her day, making it a potpourri of all the ingredients her mother liked best. She was about to start with the A on her social paper but before she could begin, Helen said, "Jessica is involved in secret activities. You may think she's cutting out paper dolls but actually she's probably plotting to blow up city hall."

"That's not funny, Helen," Mom said.

"I don't mean to be funny," Helen said. "Jessica's got some heavy secrets nobody else knows about. That's what she told me, didn't you, Jess?"

"You know, Helen," said Mom, "Jessica may be only ten and a half, but she's still a person, and you often say thoughtless things that make her feel bad."

"Big deal!" Helen said. "What's so terrible about Jessica having some deep, dark secrets of her own?"

"Come on, Helen," Dad said, forgetting to sulk.

"There is nothing wrong with Jessica having secrets," Mom said in her patient voice. "I'm sure we *all* have secrets that we don't care to share with others. I hope, Helen, that you feel your father and I have always respected your right to privacy."

"Ha!" said Helen, standing up and pushing away her plate. "A person has as much privacy in this family as a sardine in a sardine can."

"Oh, stop it, Helen!" Dad said. "Can't we have a peaceful dinner for a change?"

"I'd like that fine," Helen yelled, "but Mom won't ever stop prying. 'Where did you go? What do you think? Who did you talk to?' Well, I've got plenty of secrets that I'm keeping to myself because Mom has absolutely no respect for anybody's privacy, including Jessica's. And I think you have some nerve interfering in Arabella's life. She's a grown woman, not a baby, and she doesn't need either of you to tell her how to live."

Helen stamped off, and, naturally, banged the door of her room as loud as she could.

"It's just hopeless," Mom said. "I guess they have to feel their oats. Arabella got a little difficult too, but not like this. I just don't know if I can stand it for another year."

"If you just wouldn't notice every little thing, Sonja," Dad said. "Try to let some things pass. She's such a marvelous kid! And if we have to put up with a little irritability and a little show of independence along the way, it's worth it. Sonja—are you listening?"

"Of course I am, Alex," Mom said thoughtfully, looking at Jessica. "But I wonder what she meant, Jessica, when she said you and she had all those secrets. Do you have any idea what she meant?"

Mom's large blue eyes were troubled. It hurt Jessica knowing that Mom was upset. But even more the force of Helen's scorn disturbed her. Helen could not believe that she was capable of having secrets from Mom. Like Wendy, Helen also considered her a mama's baby. Was she? Had she been? Mom's face was still turned toward her, waiting. She loved Mom, ached for her, but knew that she needed to guard her own secrets with all the powers she had.

"No, I don't," Jessica said craftily, and launched into a description of all the instances of special recognition directed at her that day by Mr. Prince. Soon Mom's face relaxed. All was well.

riday, the note was printed in stencil letters.

ARE YOU COMING THIS AFTERNOON ?
IF YOU R NOD YOUR HEAD 3 X
DURING MATH. IF YOU R NOT DROP
YOUR MATH BOOK. I WILL BE
WATCHING.

A. S. F.

Jessica nodded her head three times as soon as Mr. Prince told them to get out their math books. Then she looked over at Randy. He was watching her, and he started bobbing his head, and crossing his eyes. Funny boy! She giggled, and glanced over at Wendy. Wendy was acting as if she wasn't looking at her even though her head was turned in that direction. Her eyes appeared to be examining something of interest above Jessica's head. Jessica smiled a mysterious smile as she refolded her note, and put it inside her pocket.

Barbara was going over to Wendy's house this afternoon. They'd been talking about it for days. Barbara was going to stay for dinner, and maybe even sleep over. Big deal! Who cared? Certainly not Jessica! Not somebody who had A.S.F. and maybe Randy Jackson and a great time to look forward to this afternoon.

"I'm going to the library," she told Mom when she got home after school.

"Oh? Is Wendy meeting you?"

"No, Mom, but it's okay." She forced a contented smile, and her mother looked at it suspiciously, and said, "Well then, I'll go along with you. I could use a few new mysteries myself."

"Oh, don't bother, Mom. I'm meeting a friend."

"Oh?"

"So you won't have to drive me."

"Which friend? Rachel?"

"That's right. We're meeting on Thirty-third, and we'll be back before five."

"Well, I could take the two of you, and maybe Rachel would like to come back with you. She could stay for dinner, and maybe even sleep over if it's all right with her mother."

"No, she can't . . . she . . . it's her father's birthday tonight, and . . . uh . . . they're all going out to dinner."

"Isn't that nice! Well, I'll take the two of you, anyway."

"No, please, Mom!" Jessica said sharply. "I don't want you to. Her mother is picking us up at the library later, and she'll drop me off."

"Oh." Mom looked disappointed. She turned her eyes away for a moment, and then looked back with a brave smile. "Maybe Rachel can come another day," she said. "I've never really talked to her but I've liked her ever since I spotted her reading *Oliver Twist* when she was in the third grade. I was room mother that year, and I guess I came in to school one day with some cupcakes—it might have been Halloween. There she was in the yard, reading. Her little hands were almost too small to hold that big book. I remember I was so surprised, I could hardly believe it."

"I remember those cupcakes," Jessica said.

"What?"

"Those Halloween cupcakes—they had orange and black icing with sprinkles. And that year, for Christmas, you made star-shaped cookies with silver balls, and for Valentine's Day, you made pink and white frosted hearts, and for Easter . . ."

Mom sighed. "I loved being room mother, but it really wasn't fair being such a hog. I did it for the first, second, and third grades, and then I knew I should give somebody else a chance. Other mothers enjoy doing it too."

". . . you made little rabbit cookies with peppermint pink eyes, lying in a bed of jelly beans. Mrs. Lucas, she's room mother now—she only brought chocolate chip cookies, store-bought ones, in for our class Halloween party. Oh Mom, there's no one like you."

She dropped into her mother's lap, and hugged her so hard that Mom laughed out loud, and the brave smile vanished.

Satisfied, Jessica trotted off to the library. She hated when Mom looked unhappy. More and more she was beginning to feel that Mom needed to be protected. She felt guilty about lying to Mom, but mixed with the guilt was pride. She had a secret that nobody knew—not Mom, not Wendy, not anybody. In a strange way, Wendy and Mom were connected, and it was her secret that protected her from the two of them. Maybe one day, she would share the secret with both of them, or one of them, but for the time being it belonged only to her, and she felt strong and free and just a little scared.

She lumbered up the hill and hesitated in front of the stairs that led up to the library itself. I guess I'll just wait out here for a while, she decided, and settled herself down on one of the stone ledges surrounding the stairs.

From where she sat, she could look up the street, and down the street. No one in sight. She also couldn't help looking across the street at Wendy's house. When they were friends, it was fun having the library so close. Sometimes, they'd bring home armfuls of books, and spend a marathon reading afternoon.

They were up there now, the two of them, in

Wendy's room. She could see backs. They were sitting in the big window seat, maybe playing hearts. Well, who cared! She fingered her poison locket, and thought about Barbara, silly, stupid Barbara, wearing Wendy's poison locket. But maybe Wendy just loaned her the locket. Maybe she said, "You can wear it for a week, then you have to give it back." Lots of times, she and Wendy had traded clothes or jewelry. But never their poison lockets. She felt her throat tightening, and she also knew, without exactly seeing, that they were watching her from the window.

Quickly she pulled out one of the notes, and looked up and down the block in an exaggerated way. Out of the corner of her eye, she was aware of movement at the window, of faces peering at her. She leaned forward, and concentrated deeply on a figure moving up the hill. If only it could be Randy —but, no, it turned out to be a young boy, chewing gum.

More movement at the window. Now what if that window opened, and Wendy leaned out and called her. Well, she'd have to pretend she hadn't known they were there, act surprised, astonished. And what if Wendy was smiling, and looking friendly? Why, she guessed she could smile too, but she didn't have to look all that friendly—at first. And what if Wendy said, "Come on up, Jess, and we'll all play hearts or Monopoly." What then? Well, she might tell them she was waiting for a friend or she might not. But what if Wendy kept begging her, "Come on, Jess, don't be like that. We really need you." What if . . .

She could sense a quietness suddenly at the window, and she stole a quick look. The window shade was drawn. Wendy had pulled down the shade and closed her out.

She pulled out her two notes, and pretended to be engrossed in them. Her cheeks burned, and she had to breathe deeply a couple of times to keep from crying. How mean they were—especially Wendy! No—not Wendy! It was Barbara. How she hated Barbara!

Think about Randy, she told herself. Where was he, anyway? Would he come? Have a look inside. No point in sitting outside any longer. Well, did she really think she was going to find Randy inside? It was all beginning to cave in around her when she saw Barbara come out of Wendy's house and head across the street toward her.

Barbara was smiling but not exactly smiling. At least, she wasn't smiling at Jessica. Her eyes were floating around in every other direction except in Jessica's, and the smile seemed lost and uncertain.

Jessica flung a fierce, hating look at her. Although Barbara's eyes were still roaming, she must have felt the force of that look because she stopped and hesitated.

"Well?" Jessica hissed. "What do *you* want?"

Barbara stood on one leg. Down the front of her shirt hung the poison locket. She reached up a finger and nervously poked at it. "Hi, Jessica," she said weakly. For one moment her eyes met Jessica's and then, quickly, she looked away.

"What do you want?" Jessica demanded.

"Well . . . I . . . Wendy sent me."

"What does she want?" A faint stirring of hope began rising inside Jessica.

"She says . . . look, Jessica, this was her idea not mine . . . but she says you should stop spying on her."

"Well . . ." Jessica had to stop for a moment to choke back her anger. Then it all came out anyway in a fierce, painful rush. "You . . . you must feel really proud of yourself—taking away my friend, and making fun of me, and pulling down the shade, and saying all those mean things about me behind my back. It must make you feel great!"

"No, no, I didn't," said Barbara, looking earnestly at her and moving slowly closer.

Jessica sniffed, and the tears began falling.

"No, honest, I didn't," said Barbara. "She didn't want to be friends with you any more. She said you made her feel bad. I never took her away from you. She was the one who stopped being friends with you. I didn't have anything to do with it."

"I made *her* feel bad! That's really funny," wept Jessica. "She was the one who made me feel bad. She was the one who always picked the fights. She was the one who always made me say I was sorry even though it was always her fault. You can ask anyone. Ask the kids in the class. Ask my mother. Ask her mother."

"She says you're a goody-goody, a mama's baby. She says you even make her mother mad at her. She says you always act like you're better than anybody else, and she just got sick of having everybody think she was the bad one and you were the good one. She says you're boring, and she always had to think up all the ideas for what you did together . . ."

"It's not true. It's not true." Jessica was really crying hard now. "It was my idea to buy the lockets, and you . . . why did you make her give you the locket. She and I swore we'd never stop wearing them, and then you . . ."

"No, I didn't!" Barbara was looking at her in a worried way. She moved in again a little closer. Jessica tried to move also but now the ledge stopped her. "She made me take it. I didn't want it but she said if I wanted to be her friend, I'd have to wear it every day."

"Because she wants me to feel bad," Jessica yelled. "That's why she told you to wear it every day. She doesn't like you at all. She just hates me more."

"Maybe," Barbara said thoughtfully. "She sure does hate you, I guess." She put up her hand, and touched the locket. "She sure is a mean one." Barbara shook her head from side to side, and then added weakly, "But it's fun being with her. The things she thinks up!"

"I know, I know," Jessica wailed. "I want to be friends again, but she won't, and I don't know what to do. What should I do?"

As soon as she said what should I do, she realized how stupid she was being, asking Barbara—her enemy, Barbara—what to do.

Barbara moved even closer, and now there was no place to go at all. They both sat down side by side on the ledge. "Listen, Jessica," she said, putting her hand on Jessica's, "she's one lousy friend to you. I guess maybe she's even jealous of you because you're really not mean and she is. You don't need her."

"Thanks a lot," Jessica said bitterly, pulling her hand away. "Last person I need advice from is you."

"Okay, have it your own way."

"Does . . . does Wendy tell you a lot of bad things about me?"

There must have been so much hurting in Jessica's eyes that Barbara hesitated, and then looked away.

"Who cares," Jessica cried. "I don't even want her for a friend any more. I've got a better friend, and that's who I'm waiting for right now."

Barbara brightened. "No kidding, Jessica, are you really waiting for a friend?"

"I told you I was."

"Is it the one who's been writing you the notes? Wendy can't stand it that somebody's sending you secret notes and not her."

Jessica wiped away at some of the wet spots on her cheeks. She felt better suddenly. "Wendy wants to know who it is, doesn't she? Well, you can tell her that the reason I'm here today," Jessica waved the note around, "is because A.S.F. asked me to come. It has nothing to do with her."

Barbara chuckled. "She thought maybe it was Randy Jackson so she asked him today if he was doing it."

Jessica's knees began trembling but she managed to look unconcerned.

"So?" she asked coldly.

"So he said it wasn't him. He said—well, never mind what he said. Anyway, then he and Wendy started kidding around, and she said he should drop over to her house today, and she'd play him her new Fleetwood Mac record."

"He . . . he's there now?" Jessica whispered.

"Sure. Didn't you see him before? Look, there are the two of them looking out the window."

Jessica did not look. She had to control a wild desire to get up and run—fast—away from Wendy's window.

"Anyway, he doesn't know who it is either, and she really wants to know. Maybe if you told her she might even be friends with you again."

Wearily, Jessica stood up. "Do me a favor," she said to Barbara.

"Sure, Jessica, and listen, don't say if you don't want to. I'm glad you've got a friend you like, and I . . . I don't really believe all those stories Wendy says about you. But what's the favor?"

Barbara was smiling at her. She had even white teeth, and large dimples in her cheeks. Her skin was very dark and very smooth. Jessica wanted to say, "Tell Wendy to drop dead, and you too." But Barbara was smiling at her, and as much as she hated Barbara, she could not say it.

Instead she turned and fled upstairs into the sanctuary of the library. Hopelessly, she inspected the groups of kids in the children's room. What was she expecting to happen anyway? Wendy had struck again, and as usual, she was the loser. Why not just give up? There was nothing she could do or say. Wendy would never be her friend again, and maybe nobody else would either. Was she as dull and boring as Wendy said? Did Wendy see her as she saw Rachel Ross? What about the notes? They had failed her too, hadn't they? There was no secret friend! And nobody knew that better than Jessica.

She sat down at one of the tables and wondered what to do next. A whole empty, lonely weekend stretched out in front of her. Mama's baby, Wendy said she was. Was she? She was trying not to be, but a great longing came over her to run home as fast as she could, leap into Mom's lap and tell her everything.

"Jessica!"

She looked up. Linda Hall was standing there, breathing hard, as if she'd been running.

"I'm so out of breath. My mother made me run some errands for her."

Jessica straightened up, and began feeling better. Linda Hall, at least, liked her. Linda had always liked her.

"Did you get your books yet?" Linda asked. "Wait for me and we'll walk home together."

Jessica thought—yesterday when the note arrived telling me to meet A.S.F. at the library, had Linda seen it? No, it certainly did not seem as if she had. Or had she? But see, here she was.

"I've got to start my report on explorers," Linda said, taking off her coat. "Which one did you take? Cortez?"

"Yes, Cortez," said Jessica thoughtfully. Interesting that Linda knew she was doing a report on Cortez. Very interesting! What else did Linda know about her? She wasn't at all surprised to see her at the library. Of course, the reason she was late was because her mother had made her run some errands. That's why she was so out of breath. She must have run all the way. Maybe she knew that Jessica would be waiting. Maybe there really *was* a secret friend in Jessica's life. Maybe the name of that friend was going to be Linda Hall.

"I guess I'd better see which explorers are left. You're not ready to go yet, are you?"

"No, no!" said Jessica. "Take your time. I'll wait for you."

"Great!" Linda's smile was warm and very friendly. It would have to be Linda and not Randy. Too bad, but Linda was a nice girl, a friendly girl, and if she turned out to be A.S.F., well, it was better than nothing.

She walked over to Linda who was balancing a book on Ponce de Leon in one hand, and another on Balboa in the other.

"What do you think, Jessica?"

"It doesn't make any difference," Jessica told her, "they're both boring."

Linda flipped through the pages of the book on Ponce de Leon. "Eighty-nine pages," she reported. Then she looked at the one on Balboa. "Eighty-three." She put the book on Ponce de Leon back on the shelf, and carried the other book to the table. "Maybe I'll take a couple of fun books out too. Read anything good lately?"

"What kind of books do you like?"

"About girls."

"That's easy."

They spent some time checking out their likes and dislikes. Linda ended up with six books, and Jessica took only three—all Rosemary Sutcliff's. She hugged them to her, as they walked home together. Linda lived only two blocks away from her. It was pleasant walking with Linda, and not very surprising when Linda asked suddenly, "Did you ever find out who your secret friend was?"

"Yes, I did," said Jessica. She looked earnestly at Linda, and noted how her eyes blinked quickly several times.

"Do you want to say?"

"Well," Jessica said, smiling warmly at her, "I guess that person knows who he/she is, and when that person is ready to say who he/she is, then I guess I'll be able to say too."

Linda nodded, and was silent.

"Would you like to come over to my house tomorrow?" Jessica asked.

"Oh, I'd love to," Linda said sadly, "but I'm supposed to spend the day with my grandmother, and sleep over her house. I hate to go. She's always telling me to clean my nails. But anyway, I'll be back Sunday. Are you free Sunday?"

"I think so."

"Well, why don't I call you Sunday morning when I get back?"

"That sounds okay."

Linda turned off on her street, and Jessica continued on to hers. She couldn't wait for Sunday. She was suddenly hungry for friendship—any friendship. If it couldn't be Wendy or Randy, well then Linda would do or somebody else—anybody. Just for a moment the memory of Randy behind the window, probably laughing behind her back with Wendy, made her throat tighten. Well, she didn't need him any more. She didn't need Wendy either. The problem of A.S.F. was solved. Now she'd have a friend again, a friend to visit and to hang out with at school. Oh, how she needed a friend! A real friend, one that others could see as well as herself. What a good day this had turned out to be after all!

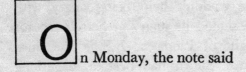

Chapter Seven

On Monday, the note said

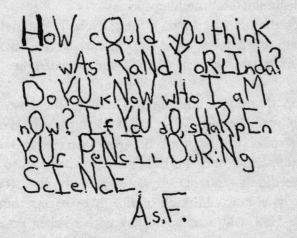

This time, every other letter was written in a high, angular style, and each alternate letter was printed square and chunky.

She hated Randy now, as well as Barbara. She hated Wendy too, and wondered what kinds of things Wendy must be telling them about her. She felt prickles of embarrassment thinking about what a wealth of secrets Wendy had to choose from—secrets whispered over the past five years. She'd told Wendy everything. She'd trusted Wendy just as if Wendy was Mom. Wendy had the combination to all her sore, private places, and she knew Wendy was sharing them with Barbara and maybe even Randy.

And Linda—she couldn't help being angry with Linda. Maybe she should be angry at herself too for ever having thought of Linda as A.S.F. She must have been desperate. But it had been a long, long weekend, and she had hoped that Sunday might be the beginning of something special.

Not that it was Linda's fault. Nobody could help getting the chicken pox. But she would be out the rest of the week just when Jessica needed her the most.

This morning while she was writing the note, she thought to herself, why am I doing this? Wendy won't make up, so stop! But she was feeling lonely and desperate, and she didn't know what else to do. If she didn't send herself notes, nobody else would. Nobody else would even notice her—except maybe Linda Hall, who was home sick with chicken pox.

People noticed the notes though. Linda did, and so did Wendy, Barbara, and Randy. Maybe others were noticing too. Maybe somewhere in her class there was somebody who was waiting to be her friend. Why not? Somewhere in that class of thirty-one kids there had to be someone. It was only a question of finding him/her out—like a treasure hunt.

Jessica looked around the room and wondered who. She flattened the note out with her hand, and let her eyes float—past Wendy, past Barbara, past Rachel Ross, past Linda's empty seat, past Randy Jackson. There! See how easy it was. She had eliminated five out of thirty-one. Counting herself, that made six. Six out of thirty-one was about one fifth— only four fifths to go. Somewhere in that four fifths of thirty-one was her friend.

And she might as well exclude Anita Loomis, who didn't like her, and Susie Frankel, whom she didn't like. Add Susie Edelstein, who caught her laughing when Wendy called her "Frankenstein," and Robert Say, who bit her once in second grade.

There now. That made ten out of thirty-one—or one third who had already been eliminated. Only twenty-one to go. And three were absent—so that made nineteen, because she had already eliminated Linda Hall. This was turning out to be a lot easier than she had thought.

By the end of the day, Jessica had narrowed the field to five—Jeff Choy, Ben Pepper, Lori Chu, Amy Thomas, and Paula Petrakis. She considered carefully the qualifications of each. Jeff was good-natured and outgoing, Ben Pepper was the best-looking boy in the class, Lori Chu was smart, Amy Thomas was pretty, and Paula Petrakis could kick the ball better than anybody else.

Perhaps Amy could be eliminated, since she and Jessica never seemed to have much to say to one another, and she guessed, regretfully, that Jeff Choy would have to go too, since he was Randy Jackson's best friend.

So that by the end of the day, only three contenders remained in the field. Jessica sharpened her pencil as the note suggested. She determined to observe each of the finalists narrowly in the next day or two before making a selection.

Barbara came up to her after math. Barbara's face was wrinkled in distaste, and she said quickly, "Wendy wants her things back."

Jessica blinked, and looked at her without understanding.

"You know—her sweater and the eyebrow pencil and the Love's Fresh Lemon Body Mist."

"Oh—I forgot."

"Look, that's all right. I'll tell her." Barbara seemed in a hurry to go, but Jessica snapped at her, "Why doesn't she ask me herself? Why does she have you do her dirty work?"

Barbara tried to smile. It was a weak, unwilling smile and it had a familiar look to it. Of course, it was her old smile, the same unwilling smile she had smiled all the time she and Wendy were friends, and Wendy made her join in doing things she didn't want to do.

Helen was in her room when Jessica arrived home after school. This was the day that Mom and Dad were going to Berkeley, and wouldn't be home until dinnertime. Helen had books and papers all over her desk and hardly answered when Jessica said "Hi!"

Jessica stood in the doorway, studying her sister's back. It would be good to talk to someone, anyone, even Helen, anyone—except Mom. Helen must have felt those eyes on her back because she turned sharply and said, "Well? What do you want?"

"Are you busy?"

"No, I'm just sitting here in this pile of books and papers because I like to," Helen snapped.

"Oh."

"I have a test in European history tomorrow, and I also have a paper due for my American Novel class," Helen explained in a more patient voice.

"Oh."

Helen turned back to her work, but Jessica remained standing there in the doorway, looking at her sister's back with longing. In a few moments Helen turned again, and said, "What is it, Jessica? Why are you standing there? If you have something to say, spit it out."

"It's about friends."

"Friends?"

"Yes, friends."

"Well, that's hardly my department," said Helen. "Right now I don't have any time for friends, and even when I do," she continued ruefully, "they don't always have time for me."

"They don't have time for me either."

"But what about Wendy?"

"We're not friends any more."

"That's good," said Helen. "I never liked her anyway. So what's your problem?"

"Well, there are some kids in school I'm thinking about," Jessica confided. "Who would you pick for a friend between somebody good-looking, somebody smart, and somebody who's a good kicker?"

"Are you kidding?"

"No."

Helen burst out laughing, but then she put down her pencil, and turned around completely in her chair so that she was facing Jessica all the way. "As I explained, I'm hardly an expert and I'm not sure you know what you're talking about, but it seems to me that there are some other aspects to friendship besides looks, intelligence, and kicking."

"Like what?" Jessica came into the room, and sat down on Helen's bed.

"Well, first of all, it's not only you picking a friend, somebody has to pick you too. And then— friends should have common interests or at least common attitudes. And last but not least, a friend should also support you and help you out when you need help."

None of which was true in her friendship with Wendy. She and Wendy hadn't picked each other for friends. Their mothers had. They certainly didn't have common attitudes, and Wendy often made her feel bad.

"Okay?"

"Okay," Jessica said with admiration. "You know so much, Helen, I don't know why you don't have lots and lots of friends."

"I guess it's not so easy to practice what you preach," Helen sighed. She looked thoughtfully at Jessica and said, "Listen, Jess, I'm sorry if I was mean the other day when I told about you having secrets, and I apologize. But Mom gets me so mad sometimes I say things I'm sorry for later. I didn't mean to hurt your feelings, and I'm sorry if I did."

"That's all right, Helen. I didn't really mind. But don't you love Mom?"

"I guess so, but I don't love the way she's always breathing down my neck."

Jessica nodded. Mom had been breathing down her neck too, she guessed, just as Helen said, but she didn't feel angry at Mom the way Helen did. Sometimes she felt irritated, but more and more she was feeling sorry for Mom, and she didn't know why.

"Well, don't you think mothers are supposed to be interested in their kids?" she said loyally.

"Not like Mom," Helen snorted. "The trouble with her is that she doesn't have enough outside interests. She's around the house too much."

"She's writing the cookbooks," said Jessica. "People consider her an authority on cooking."

"Cooking!" said Helen scornfully.

"Well, what's wrong with cooking?" said Jessica, aware of a growing chasm at the bottom of her stomach. She wondered anxiously (although she kept it to herself) what was going to be for dinner.

"There's nothing wrong with cooking, in its place," said Helen, "but today a woman has to be more than a housewife or she'll run into trouble. Look, Jessica, I'd really like to discuss this further with you. It's good to know you're thinking these days, but right now I've got to study. So get out of here and let me work."

Jessica basked in the warmth of her sister's praise. Helen was always sparing with her compliments. The moment was too precious to waste.

"Helen," she said.

"What?"

"Can I come in here and read?"

"Sure," said Helen amiably, "if you can manage to keep your mouth shut and leave me alone."

It was good sitting in Helen's room and watching Helen's back. It was cozy too, curled up on Helen's bed, reading and listening to the comforting sounds of rustling paper and Helen grumbling to herself. How independent Helen was, and strong-minded! Would she ever be like Helen? She didn't think so. Helen usually made up her mind and stuck to it, while she could change her mind over and over again in one day.

Helen didn't seem to need friends either, the way she did. Maybe Helen's suggestions would help though. Maybe tomorrow she might apply them to the three finalists. One of them was bound to qualify.

Around six, they heard the outside door open and their parents' voices in the hallway.

"Hello, hello," Mom yelled cheerfully, coming up the stairs and into the room. She paused by Helen's desk, bent over and picked up a few papers on the floor. "Oh, what a day, and am I tired!"

"Am I hungry!" said Dad, following her in and dropping into a chair. He seemed cheerful too. They both seemed cheerful. Jessica wondered if at this very moment Arabella was cheerful too.

"Did you see Arabella?" she asked. "Is she still going around with that old guy?"

Mom laughed good-naturedly. "Arabella's fine, and she sends her love. Oh, we had the nicest lunch —one of those real cute restaurants where the students hang out. Lots of plants all over the place, and health breads. There was an earwig in my fruit salad and . . . oh, my feet are killing me." She bent over and eased off a copper-colored shoe with dark green stacked heels. She pouted down at her foot, and she looked to Jessica like a little girl. She was wearing a dark green velveteen pantsuit with a green and white plaid blouse that had a very large bow in front. Her face looked small and innocent above the large bow. Suddenly Jessica felt so sorry for her that she hurried over and kissed her. Mom was pleased. She pulled her down and murmured, "How's my baby doll?"

"Oh, just fine, Mom."

"Did you have a nice day?"

"Just fine, Mom. Did you see Arabella?"

"Sure we saw Arabella, and we had a nice, long chat," Mom cooed, "and . . ."

"And?" Jessica urged. "What about that old guy?"

"His name, Jessica, is Dr. Petersen," said Dad,

"and I can assure you he was not the main topic of conversation."

"No," Mom agreed, "he was not." She looked at Dad's cheerful face, and then burst out laughing. "At least, he wasn't after Arabella told us he was planning to get married to one of the women in the chamber group."

"Married!" said Helen with disgust.

"Yes, isn't that nice?" Mom kicked off her other shoe. "Dr. Petersen sounds like a lovely person and a very fine teacher. He and Arabella have become such good friends too. It seems he was impressed with Arabella's musicianship—and when he heard her play her flute, he thought she might like to join the chamber group. So that's why he took her there. I can't tell you how highly I think of him."

"But yesterday you called him a predatory old goat. I heard you tell Dad that's what he was," snapped Helen.

"I never said such a thing," Mom protested, "but anyway, I understand that his fiancée . . ."

"Fiancée!" Helen said with loathing.

". . . is a charming woman about thirty-three who plays the oboe. Well, after that I went to Kroeber Hall, and the exhibit was marvelous. I never saw such a collection of sieves in my life, and from all over the world."

"What's for dinner," Jessica moaned, returning to basics.

"There's some Flemish beef stew I'll have to heat

up, and I'll make a salad, but I think we may be out of lettuce. I just haven't been myself these last couple of days. Oh, I'm so tired I can hardly move."

"Why don't we all go out for pizza tonight?" Dad suggested. "It's too late to start fussing."

"Pizza!" Helen said approvingly.

"Okay by me, let's go!" Jessica cried.

"I don't mind," said Mom. "Tonight I could even eat pizza, I'm feeling so good."

"This is some day," said Dad. "I actually found something we all agree on at the same time."

Chapter Eight

There was a note lying right in the middle of her desk Tuesday morning. It was on a large, dirty piece of gray construction paper, folded in half. Astonished, she picked it up but before opening it, looked suspiciously around the classroom. Most of the kids were hanging up their sweaters and jackets. A few were sitting at their desks. Barbara was talking to Mr. Prince. And Wendy? Where was Wendy? She couldn't find her anywhere even though she had been out in the yard earlier.

Jessica opened the note cautiously. It said:

> The time has come to
> tell you who I am.
> I love you and my name is
>   Freddie Arnold
> P.S. Meet me in front of
> The Boys' ROOM after
> school, and we will seal
> our friendship with a kiss.

The handwriting was purposely messy. Now some-body began making choking sounds. She whirled around and saw Wendy moving out from behind the reading corner. Wendy was pretending to look inno-cent but her face and shoulders were shaking with the effort to hold back her laughter. Jessica began tearing up the note—once, twice, three times, four . . . until she couldn't tear any more. Then she gathered all the pieces together, and threw them out in the wastebasket near Mr. Prince's desk.

Later, in the yard, Barbara came up to her. "It was Wendy's idea," she said quickly. "I didn't have anything to do with it."

"Who cares!" Jessica said.

Ben Pepper and Jeff Choy were busy dissecting a sand shark that Ben's father had brought in for class. Paula Petrakis hadn't looked her way all morning, and during recess, she, Amy Ashimura and Jack Ryan had a three-way rubber-band fight. It was likely that Paula would be eliminated shortly if she did not mend her ways. Lori Chu, on the other hand, had smiled at her when she admired Lori's sci-ence report.

"I told her I didn't even think it was funny," Bar-bara explained. The poison locket hung conspicuously down her front.

"Sure, sure!"

"I really did, Jessica, and listen, I was think-ing . . ."

"Well, good for you." Jessica's tone was nasty but

Barbara overlooked it. "Did your friend come?"

"What friend?"

"You know—A.S.F.—at the library on Friday? We took turns watching, and we only saw Jackie Ellison, Linda Hall, and Ben Pepper."

"So?"

"Was it one of them?"

"I'm not going to tell *you*."

"Okay, but listen—I was thinking. If it wasn't one of them, I was wondering if A.S.F. might be . . ."

"Who?" Jessica's knees began trembling.

Barbara lowered her voice. "I was wondering if it might be Wendy."

"Wendy?"

"Sure. She'd be mean enough to tell you to go to the library, and never show up. See what I mean?"

"That's crazy."

"I don't know what the notes say, but maybe she wants to tease you and that's why she's writing them."

"You've got it all wrong," said Jessica. "The person who's writing the notes is my friend, and that person wants me to be happy, and would never make fun of me or tease me. A friend is someone who supports you and helps you out when you need help."

"That's right," agreed Barbara, "so who was it on Friday?"

Jessica considered for a moment. Then she swallowed and admitted, "Nobody came. Maybe something happened, or maybe"—she looked right at Barbara—"A.S.F. knew you three were spying and didn't want to be seen."

Barbara reached up and touched her locket just the same way Wendy always used to do when they were friends. Barbara was right. Wendy was mean, and every time she saw that locket hanging on Barbara she'd never forget just how mean Wendy was.

"Well," Barbara said slowly, "why wouldn't A.S.F. tell you?"

"How do you know he hasn't?"

"Is it a he?"

"Or she hasn't?"

"Well . . ." Barbara leaned over and whispered in Jessica's ear, "I still think it's Wendy. She's always talking about the notes. You watch out. If she's doing it, you just watch out. She's so mean—she'd do anything."

"Well, if you think she's so mean," Jessica said, "why are you friends with her? I always knew she was mean when we were friends, but I didn't care—as long as she wasn't mean to me."

"She's fun," said Barbara weakly.

"I know," Jessica agreed.

"But mean people—sooner or later they turn on you."

"Maybe," said Jessica, "but we were friends for five years, and she was mean to lots of other people but not usually to me."

"I guess she finally ran out of victims," suggested Barbara.

They both giggled, and then stopped.

Jessica said stiffly, "Well, if you think she's so mean you don't have to be her friend."

"I know," said Barbara, "I don't really like the things she says and the way she's always making fun of other kids. I don't really like it."

"Well," said Jessica, moving a little closer, "one day she'll turn on you."

"I know," said Barbara.

The two of them touched their lockets and considered.

"If you were smart you wouldn't wait until something awful happened like with me. Just look at me. I haven't got any friends. I'm a mess."

"You've got A.S.F."

"Yes, but . . ."

"Barbara!" shrieked Wendy from the tether-ball court.

"If I were you," said Jessica, "I'd get out while I could. You're not such a mean kid, I guess. Probably there would be lots of kids in the class who would like you."

"Barbara!"

"Who, for instance?"

"Well, maybe Rachel Ross."

"She's stupid!"

"Rachel Ross is stupid! How can you say such a thing? She reads *all* the time."

"I know, but she's stupid. Did you ever try talking to her?"

"Yes, but she reads . . . yes . . . you know, I think you're right. She is stupid but I don't think anybody knows that except us."

They smiled at each other. "But don't tell anyone," said Barbara, "because it would be mean to make fun of her. After all, she can't help herself being stupid. That's why she reads all the time."

"Barbara!"

"Well, I guess I better go. She's been calling me."

"You don't have to go."

"I know, but . . ."

"Barbara!"

Barbara suddenly leaped up, and began hurrying off. "Just remember what I said about *her,*" she yelled over her shoulder, "and watch out!"

Jessica leaned back against the wall, and watched her go. Wendy was waiting for her on the tether-ball court. Wendy began talking hard and fast when Barbara rushed up, and Barbara just stood there, listening. Big-mouth Wendy! Look at that dope, Barbara, standing there, just taking it—the way *she* used to take it. What a turkey that Barbara was! At least nobody was picking on *her* any more.

She looked around the yard. Jeff, Randy, and Lori Chu were playing volleyball with Susie, Ben Pepper, and Alan. Other kids were running, talking, laughing, joking. She was sitting all alone. Even though nobody was picking on her, she was sitting all alone. It was terrible.

She worked on a new note and tucked it into her

art folder. It was right there on top when she opened it. This time the writing was round and thick, and had been done with yellow- and purple-ink pens.

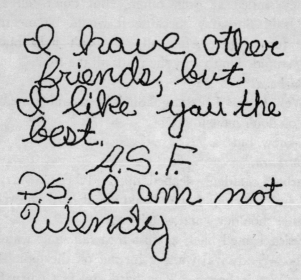

I have other
friends, but
I like you the
best.
          A.S.F.
P.S. I am not
Wendy

There now! She considered showing the note to Barbara, but an opportunity never arose. Her lonely feeling persisted, and even reading the note over a few times did not help. She forgot to check out Ben Pepper, Lori Chu, and Paula Petrakis.

During afternoon gym, Barbara was one of the team captains for kickball. She picked Wendy first, Randy Jackson, second, and Jessica third.

"Why did you pick her?" she could hear Wendy hiss.

"She's a pretty fast runner," Barbara said weakly.

"Are you kidding? She never even manages to kick the ball."

"Shh! She'll hear."

"Who cares?"

The first time Jessica was up she kicked a weak little fly ball right into Karen Yves's arms. The next time, she could hear Wendy groaning behind her. There were two players on base—Barbara at second and Alan at third. Wendy kept groaning. Jessica took a deep breath, and when the ball came toward her, she thought—that ball is Wendy, and she kicked as hard as she could. The ball shot out right between the pitcher and first base.

"Run, run!" she could hear her teammates shout as she touched first.

"Keep going!"

She scrambled into second, just in time to see the ball whizzing home. Barbara was coming in from third, and she had to duck down to keep from getting tagged. She slipped and fell but managed to touch home safe. When she stood up, her sweater and pants were dirty from the fall.

Randy Jackson was up next, and he kicked a double, bringing Jessica home.

"Nice work," Barbara said enthusiastically.

As Jessica walked toward her teammates, she suddenly noticed it on the ground, about ten feet to the side, away from home. She looked quickly at Barbara. The locket was not around her neck. Evidently it had become unfastened during her fall, and lay there now, glinting in the sun. Any minute, somebody else would spot it. Any minute, Barbara would miss her locket. Carefully, she began moving. Nobody noticed. She put her foot right on it, lightly, and then bent down and pretended to tie her shoe. She slipped her fingers carefully under her shoe, and let them close over the locket. When she stood up, nobody was looking at her, and she was able to slide the locket into her pocket.

"My locket," Barbara yelled suddenly when they were back in the classroom. "I lost my locket."

Mr. Prince asked all the kids to look around for it, and Jessica not only checked under her desk, and near the door, but made a special point of looking long after everybody else had stopped.

Home in her room that afternoon, Jessica gloated. She spread the captured locket out on her desk, and considered the various alternatives.

1) She could put red poison in it that looked like Jello, and return it to Barbara. She would not return it personally, but she could leave it someplace where Barbara would be sure to find it. That way, nobody could blame her when Barbara died of poisoning.

2) She could take it over to Wendy's house and say she had found it. No, wait! Better to say that somebody else had found it and returned it to her, Jessica, believing it was hers. Maybe if she could get Wendy alone, or even with Gloria, then maybe they could make up and become friends again. She felt a little ashamed of herself for thinking about making up with Wendy again, but the opportunity was too good to pass up.

3) Throw the locket out after stamping on it.

She went over each alternative but could not come to a final decision. No hurry, she thought to herself as long as I have the locket and Barbara doesn't.

She was singing when she came downstairs into the kitchen. Mom was inspecting three or four crabs wriggling around in the sink. She looked over at Jessica, and smiled. "You sound happy," she said.

"I am." Jessica stood next to her and peered down into the sink. "What are you doing with those crabs?"

"Getting them ready for their debut in tonight's dinner."

"Oh? What's for dinner?"

"Cioppino."

"Cioppino?"

"Yes, it's a dish that originated here in San Francisco by Portuguese fishermen. Tonight we're having a California dinner—cioppino, garbanzo and kidney bean salad, sourdough french bread and cheesecake à la Fresno for dessert."

"Yum!"

"Grandma's coming, and so are Uncle Jay and Aunt Carol. Maybe you'd like to set the dining-room table for me when you get a chance."

"Sure, Mom, and can I do anything else?" She rubbed up against her mother, and leaned her head on Mom's shoulder.

Mom bent down and kissed her. "Just keep on

singing," she said. "That's the best kind of help. Are you and Wendy friends again?"

"No, Mom, but it's all right."

"If you like," Mom said, "you could have a slumber party, and invite some friends, including Wendy . . ."

"But it's not my birthday."

"Well, what about a holiday party?"

"What holiday? It's November. Nothing important happens in November except for Thanksgiving, and nobody has Thanksgiving parties."

"What about Veterans Day, or . . ."

"Mom!" Jessica's voice was sharper than she meant it to be. "I don't want a party. Forget about it." Mom blinked, and turned back to the crabs.

"I mean, I don't think it would do any good," Jessica continued, looking at her mother's back. "I mean, it's a good idea. Maybe another time . . ."

"That's all right, Jessie," said Mom, just a little stiffly.

"You know the kids love to come here," Jessica soothed, edging closer. She put out a finger, and touched a cold crab. Lately it seemed, she had to be the one who worried about protecting Mom instead of the other way around. "You always make such great goodies—all the kids talk about you."

"Well, you never seem to have anybody over," Mom said sulkily. "Why don't you ask some of your friends to come and play? Why don't you ask Rachel?"

"Oh, Rachel. Well, she lives all the way over near Twenty-third."

"She could come home with you, and I'd drive her home. I don't know why you never ask her. You seem to be spending a lot of time with her at school. Why don't you ever bring her home?"

One of the crabs took a quick snap at Jessica's finger, and she pulled it away and yelled. Mom started laughing, and Jessica took a deep breath. More and more she was feeling sorry for Mom, sorry for something that was happening that she could not help.

"Okay, Mom," she said vaguely, "I'll ask her over one day."

Mom lifted the crabs onto a wooden board. "When?"

"Oh—whenever she can make it."

"Don't make it tomorrow."

"Okay."

"I'll be busy tomorrow."

"Sure, Mom."

"Thursday or Friday would be fine."

"I'll ask her but . . ."

"And I'll make some brownies, or maybe peanut butter cookies. Which do you think she'd like better?"

"They're both great, Mom, but I wish you wouldn't . . ."

"Or maybe those pumpkin muffins you like so much—with the dates and spices."

"I don't even know if she can come, Mom."

"I'll call her mother if you think that would help."

"Please, Mom, I'll ask her. Don't call her mother. Please! I promise, I'll work it out."

"That's fine then." Mom turned her attention back to the crabs, and, exhausted, Jessica moved off to set the dining-room table.

Chapter Nine

The school buses were bright yellow, and inside, the seats were green. For the most part, only the Black kids got to ride the buses. But if you were going home with a friend who rode them, then you could ride too.

Wendy was going home with Barbara. Jessica could see them laughing together inside the group waiting for the buses to come. Randy Jackson and David Bennett were standing close by playing a noisy game of Rochambeau.

Earlier in the day, Barbara had stood over her desk while she was working on her Indian mask. She was carefully outlining the eyelids with a green marker pen, and Barbara's breathing bothered her. She looked up, right at Barbara's chest where no locket was hanging, and felt cheerful.

"Well?"

"That's really beautiful," said Barbara.

"Thank you." Loftily, Jessica returned to her mask. Today, after school, she had decided to take the locket over to Wendy's house and make one final attempt. She picked up her pen, but Barbara was still there, breathing.

"Well?"

"I think it's Wendy."

"You told me that already, and I told you it wasn't."

"It has to be her because she keeps asking around, and everybody says no, it's not them."

Jessica's knees were trembling, but she managed to say coolly, "Well, you don't think the person is going to say yes, do you? It is supposed to be a secret, after all."

"Yes, but she's asked everybody. You know what? She even asked me."

Jessica rolled her eyes skyward.

"See what I mean? Now why would she ask me?"

"She must be crazy."

"No, she knows what she's doing, that girl. She's trying to make it look like it's somebody else. She's not crazy, but she's mean as a snake, like I told you. She'll get it to look like somebody else is crazy while she's the one."

"What's so crazy," Jessica asked stiffly, "about somebody wanting to be friends with me?"

"It's not that." Barbara waved her hand impatiently. "But what kind of a kid would keep writing notes and never say who it is?"

"Somebody special," Jessica said softly. "Somebody nice and friendly and not mean."

"How about the handwriting?"

"It's always different."

"See—that proves it—it has to be Wendy. She'd know how to disguise her handwriting. She'd have it all figured out before anybody else."

"It is *not* Wendy!"

Jessica picked up her ink pen and held it poised over the eye on her mask.

Today when she brought over the locket to Wendy's house, she had it all planned out. When Wendy opened the door, she would quickly hand her the locket, and then, before Wendy could shut the door she'd tell her that she had brought all the notes with her and would like to ask Wendy's opinion. Wendy might hesitate for a moment, but Jessica knew that Wendy was even more curious about the notes than Barbara. And that was how they would make up. She knew, with absolute certainty, that Wendy would ask her to come in, would look at all the notes, and would finally come up with an opinion. Now—and she was ready—the important thing was to act as if everything Wendy said made sense. Even though it wasn't going to. No matter who she said was A.S.F., Jessica should agree. Even if she said it was Barbara. Just agree. Once they were friends again, there would be plenty of time for the truth.

Wendy was curious. Wendy was always curious, more than anybody else, and that's why the plan was going to succeed in the end. She would do anything to find out who A.S.F. was. Maybe she had even sent Barbara over to try and find out.

She looked coldly up at Barbara, and said, "I can't work with you standing over me."

"Oh!" Barbara's eyes opened very wide—hurt. She said, "Oh!" again, and then quickly moved away.

Angrily, Jessica turned back to her work. Why did Barbara keep bothering her? What a dumb idea that was about Wendy writing the notes. It was all she could do to stop herself from laughing out loud. She didn't mean to hurt Barbara's feelings, but who asked her to keep butting in?

And now Wendy was going home with Barbara, going home on the bright yellow school bus. Helplessly, Jessica stood watching. Her beautiful plan— all shot to pieces. That lousy Barbara!

"Hey, Jessica!"

Wendy was calling her, smiling at her in a friendly way. Maybe Barbara had been talking to her. Maybe they were going to invite her too. What would she do if they asked her to come along? Mom was expecting her but if they asked her, she could go, call home from Barbara's house. Mom would understand.

"Jessica!"

She licked her braces hopefully, and said, "Yes?"

"I know who A.S.F. is."

"Oh!" She guessed they weren't going to invite her after all.

"Did you hear what I said?"

Just go home, she told herself. Smile politely, and go home. If you talk to her, you'll be sorry. But the habit was too strong. Helplessly, she moved a little closer.

"Why are you like this?" she said, that inevitable whine in her voice. "What did I do? Whatever it is,

I'm sorry, Wendy. Can't we be friends again? Please!"

How she hated herself for giving in this way. Why was it that Wendy always made her act as though she was somebody else?

"You're disgusting," Wendy said, her face red and angry. She looked as if she was going to cry. "How could anybody like *you?*"

Barbara yelled, "Come on now, Wendy, here's the bus."

Randy Jackson and David Bennett were still shouting "Rochambeau" at each other, and, searching for help, she let her eyes rest on Randy.

"It's not him, I'll tell you that," Wendy said fiercely.

Jessica looked up quickly at Wendy. She licked her braces once more for courage, and felt her knees trembling.

"Not who?" she asked weakly.

The first school bus was pulling into the curb. Barbara took Wendy's arm, and said, "Come on, Wendy, let's sit in the back."

But Wendy pulled her arm away, and said in a very loud voice, "It's not Randy Jackson who's writing those weirdo notes. I know because I asked him."

They were looking at her now—Randy and David. They had stopped playing Rochambeau, and were looking right at her. Randy's face was terrifying. Randy's face was puzzled, curious, and not at all helpful. She was all alone there, among enemies.

"It's not him, but I know who it is. I've known all along. There's only one person who's weird enough to do it, only one person who's a perfect kook—just like you."

Run! Jessica said to herself, run! Don't stand there. Now they're just looking at you but in a minute she'll tell and then they'll laugh. Run! Run!

"I know who it is, too," said another voice.

"Oh, shut up," said Wendy.

"No, I won't," said Barbara, "because it's you. You're the one. You've been sending her those notes because you're mean. You want everybody to think she's a kook, and to laugh at her, but you're the one who's a kook!"

There was a sudden ripple of laughter, and Jessica turned and ran. She knew that they weren't laughing at her this time but at Wendy, and she couldn't stand that either.

But why did Wendy hate her so much? Why? If Barbara hadn't stepped in, Wendy would have humiliated her before all the kids. Why? But there was another why that suddenly became even more important. Why was she seeking out Wendy's friendship? Why was she continuing to hunger for a friend who despised her as much as Wendy did? All her plans had been directed toward winning Wendy back. Why?

As she hurried along the street, she began assembling all the bits and pieces that had been floating inside her head for weeks—and maybe years. Remembering Jeff Choy and Randy Jackson bouncing each other around in the library door made her see again just what a friendship could be. She had been trying hard to hold onto that, but her mistake had been in supposing she and Wendy could be part of it together. Helen was right—a friend had to pick you too, and Wendy certainly did not want to pick her. Maybe she did things to Wendy that hurt Wendy too. What had Wendy said to Barbara—that she was a goody-goody, and that people always sided with her? Even now, Wendy's face had been red and angry, and she looked as if she was going to cry. "You're disgusting," she said, and it was true. It was disgusting to long for friendship with someone who abused you and resented you. It was also hopeless.

Well, no more! She needed a real friend now, and she knew that it could never again be Wendy. Standing there, a few minutes back, about to be disgraced by Wendy, it had finally ended. She reached up, and felt the hard, cold surface of the locket between her fingers. One yank, and she could fracture the delicate chain. One quick tug and she could sever the cord forever.

It was no longer necessary. She felt free of Wendy at last—beautifully free. No more Wendy, ever, ever again! No more notes either and no more A.S.F.! She had a real friend in mind now—one out of the thirty-one in her class, after all. Today had developed into a splendid day—it had seen the end of an old friendship and, she hoped, the beginning of a new.

Chapter Ten

There, lying on her desk the next day, in plain sight of everyone was a note, a *real* one. Carefully, Jessica unfolded it. Mr. Prince said, "The class will be happy to wait, Jessica, while you read your daily note."

"Oh no!" she couldn't help crying out. "This isn't my daily note."

Their laughter angered her. She slammed herself down in her seat, closed her hand over the note, and did not look at it until everybody was settled back into not looking at her. Then she read

Will you meet me by the drinking fountain during gym? I have something to tell you.
Barbara

It was signed Barbara. Barbara signed it. A *real* note signed by a *real* person. She turned with a huge smile on her face to look over at Barbara. Barbara was looking back at her—but not smiling. Jessica nodded her head up and down several times, and suddenly Barbara was smiling too.

When it was time for gym, Jessica hurried down the stairs and into the yard. The kids were organizing into a game of dodge ball, but over near the drinking fountain stood a solitary figure in red, Barbara. She began running, a big smile on her face but when she came up close and saw Barbara watching her with a puzzled look, she suddenly felt shy. Everything she'd planned on saying faded from her mind. Barbara seemed to turn shy too, and for a few moments nobody said anything.

Finally Barbara started. "Let's go sit near the stairs. Nobody can hear us over there."

She followed Barbara over to the bench and sat down beside her. She was suddenly conscious of Barbara as a person and needed to see her as somebody entirely new. Carefully she slid her eyes around to Barbara's face. Barbara was frowning. She had dimples that went down deep into the middle of her smooth brown cheeks.

"You were right," Barbara said.

"Listen!" Jessica hadn't really listened to Barbara. She was overflowing with things that needed to be said, and she began. "I'm sorry I ran away yesterday. I couldn't help it but it wasn't right. I should have stayed. Was she very upset?"

"Was who upset?"

"Wendy."

Barbara laughed out loud. It really wasn't a laugh —more of a sound—the kind of *ha* sound which doesn't mean *ha-ha*—which usually means exactly the opposite.

"I mean," explained Jessica, "because all the kids were laughing at her. It wasn't right, and I thought about it all evening but I didn't know what to do."

"All the kids weren't laughing at her," said Barbara. "Where did you get that idea?"

"I heard them. When you said she was the one who was writing the notes—I heard the kids laugh at her."

"Because you ran away then. If you'd stayed, you would have seen they weren't laughing at her."

"I'm so glad."

"No," said Barbara glumly, "they were laughing at me."

"You?"

"Sure. You don't think she was going to let me get away with telling her off. She just took me apart— man—did she ever! She just said I was the one writing the notes. She always knew it was me, and she made fun of me, and then, they all started laughing at me. So I just want you to know you were right. I shouldn't have stayed friends with her because she sure turned me inside out."

"Oh, Barbara, I'm so sorry."

"Nothing to be sorry about," said Barbara. "I learned my lesson, and you'll never catch me messing around with somebody like that. See—look at her now! See—nothing's bothering her. She's got Susie Frankenstein—I mean Edelstein—hooked now. She'll always have somebody."

They both looked hard at Wendy standing in the sunshine, shaking back her long blond hair and laughing with her long white teeth.

"Mean as a snake," said Barbara sadly, "but the things she thinks up."

"I know," said Jessica sadly. "She's so much fun."

They watched Wendy in the center of the dodge-ball circle leap and laugh as the others tried to hit her with the ball.

"One day," Barbara said tenderly, "we called a whole lot of people on the telephone and said we were the missing persons bureau and did they know anything about a man called Harvey Wallbanger. And do you know, one lady said she did, and he lived upstairs."

They both laughed, and then it was Jessica's turn to reminisce. "One day, we wrote letters to people—took their names out of the phone book—and told them to meet us in front of the Russian Store on Geary on Friday at four o'clock, and wear a daisy in their coat and we'd give them ten dollars each, and you know what?" Jessica was choking with laughter.

"What? What?" Barbara was laughing too.

"We hid ourselves, and two people came. Imagine—two people came wearing daisies."

She was laughing so hard the tears were beginning to roll down her face.

"Another time," Jessica gasped, "oh . . . oh . . . I can't even talk."

They laughed together, and then they both watched Wendy, who now was one of the people in the circle.

"She'll always have friends," Jessica said. "People will always want to be friends with her."

"I guess," Barbara agreed.

"People are proud to be her friend."

"Maybe so."

"She's special."

"Well," Barbara said, "that may be, but one thing's for sure—she's not good for people like us. We can't handle ourselves with a person like Wendy. We make her worse and she makes us—nothing."

"You're right, but it sure is a pity."

"Sure is."

They watched Wendy jumping and laughing, and then Jessica licked her braces, cleared her throat, but before she could start, Barbara said, "I still think she's the one."

"What one?"

"The one who wrote the notes."

"No," said Jessica, "it wasn't Wendy."

"How can you know for sure?"

"Because I know who A.S.F. is. I've always known."

"Well, who is it?"

"You're going to hate me when I tell you."

Barbara's eyes narrowed. "I'll only hate you if you say it was me."

"No, I know it wasn't you."

"Well then, who was it?"

"It was . . . me."

"You?"

"Yes, it was me. There! Now you know the truth I guess you're really going to hate me."

Barbara's eyes searched her face. "But why?"

"Because I wanted Wendy to think I was interesting. I wanted her to be curious about me and jealous. After a while I guess I got a little mixed up myself and began pretending there really was an A.S.F. who wanted to be my friend. I almost believed that it could be different kids in the class. But at first, I was only thinking about Wendy. I figured she'd do anything to find out who wrote those notes even . . . even . . ."

"Even being your friend again?" Barbara's eyes searched out Wendy in the yard.

"Yes." Jessica could see Barbara looking thoughtfully over at Wendy. "I guess you're going to tell her. I guess you think she'll be friends with you again. I guess you'll tell all the kids. I guess . . ."

Barbara was laughing now, looking at her again, and laughing. "I guess you're a real character," Barbara said, "real sly. Wow! It was you all along, and nobody ever guessed."

"But Wendy knew. She was going to tell yesterday."

"No, she didn't." Barbara was wiping the laugh tears out of her eyes. "She was only saying that to shake you up. She didn't know."

So it was going to be all right then. Jessica licked her braces, and tried again.

"Listen, Barbara, I'll tell all the kids it wasn't you. If you want, I'll even tell them it was me. I don't want to but if you think I should I will."

"Just tell them it wasn't me. You don't have to say who it really was."

"And, Barbara, I want to tell you thanks for sticking up for me yesterday."

"Forget it," Barbara said ruefully. "I didn't do such a good job of it."

"Well, maybe if I hadn't run away I could have helped you out."

"Maybe so but it's not worth it. People like you and me, we just have to get out of the way when somebody like Wendy comes along. Because she just means trouble. Sure she's fun, but there's always somebody getting hurt on the other end. Why should we go along with that?"

"And, Barbara, I'm sorry."

"What for?"

"For yesterday when you were watching me work on my mask and I was mean to you—and other times when I was mean."

"You weren't really mean."

"And, Barbara, listen, Barbara . . ."

"I'm listening."

"I found something that belongs to you."

"Oh yeah? What?"

"Here!" She pulled the locket out of her pocket, and handed it over to Barbara.

"Oh, that!" Barbara made a face. Her dimples punched out pockets in her cheeks. "Well, I guess I'm never going to wear that again. She's not going to like me wearing it. She said she never wanted to talk to me again as long as she lived."

"Well," said Jessica carefully, "she's not the only one that locket belongs to."

Barbara looked at Jessica's face. Then she looked at Jessica's locket, hanging there right in the middle of her chest. She smiled, reached out, took up the locket, and put it around her neck. Jessica took a deep breath, leaned back against the bench, and felt happier than she'd felt in a long, long time.

"What do you like to do?" she asked softly.

"You mean after school?"

"Yes."

"All sorts of things. I like to go biking, and I like to listen to records. I like to play Ping-pong . . ."

"I know someone who has a Ping-pong table in her basement."

"Who?"

"Karen Michaelson. She lives right around the corner from me. She's only eight but I can go over and play any time I like, and I can always bring a friend. She'd love to play Ping-pong with us. You'll like her when we . . ."

It was the "we" that stopped Jessica. Barbara was silent, but somebody had to say something to make the "we" happen.

"Can you come over to my house tomorrow?" Jessica asked, carefully. "We won't have to play Ping-pong with Karen if you don't want. We can do something else."

"I guess I can come. I'll ask my mother."

"You can come Friday if tomorrow's no good. My mother's making brownies, or maybe cupcakes, or did she say cookies?"

"You mean she knows I'm coming?"

"Not exactly."

This wasn't the time to be thinking about Mom, preparing Mom for Barbara Wilson and not Rachel Ross. Would Mom approve of the substitution? Could she accept a friendship she had had no share in arranging? A sudden ache hit her when she thought of Mom and those large, trusting eyes. It was hard protecting your mother, and sometimes, Jessica knew, it might even be impossible.

"I was going to ask you if you wanted to come over to my house sometime," Barbara asked softly.

"Oh yes, I do, I want to come." She could see herself there with Barbara, laughing and joking with Barbara and the other kids, waiting for the bright yellow bus with the green seats. Did Barbara have any sisters or brothers? What kinds of food did she like? What were her favorite colors? Ahead of them stretched days and days of finding out about each other.

There was only one proper way to celebrate this beginning. She opened her notebook, and wrote, this time in her regular handwriting

Dear Barbara,
    I think we should
be grateful to Wendy.
        A.R.F.

Barbara read the note over her shoulder. "Maybe so," she said, "but what does A.R.F. stand for?"

"I'll give you a hint," said Jessica. "The 'R' stands for real."

"Then I can guess the rest," said Jessica's new friend.

About the Author

Marilyn Sachs, a native of New York City, received a Bachelor of Arts degree from Hunter College and a master's degree in library science from Columbia University. She has worked in the Brooklyn Public Library as a specialist in children's literature, and in the San Francisco Public Library. The author of over twenty-two books for young readers, she is well known for such distinguished titles as *The Bear's House*, a 1971 nominee for the National Book Award, and *Veronica Ganz*, an ALA Notable Book.

Ms. Sachs now lives with her family in San Francisco.

Look for these and other **Apple Paperbacks**
in your local bookstore!

AMY MOVES IN
Marilyn Sachs

Will Amy *ever* be happy in her new neighborhood?

At first Amy is really excited about moving. Then she begins
to realize that it's going to be harder than she thought. She
doesn't know any of the kids, there's a new school to get used
to, and on top of that, there's that mean-looking dog that lives
in her building....

But it's not easy to stay miserable for long in a neighborhood
where something exciting *always* seems to be happening!

ISBN 0-590-40254-4/$2.25 US/$2.95 CAN

LAURA'S LUCK

Marilyn Sachs

What is Laura going to do,
stuck in "the wilderness" all summer?

Laura's never been to summer camp before. She hates the
idea of leaving home and she hates sports—she's just not good
at them. Her idea of fun is reading a good book. So now that
she's been pushed into going to camp, what's she going to do?
She's convinced the other girls won't like her and that she'll
feel like a misfit.

Laura never thought, though, that there'd be girls as fun
as Anne at camp or that she'd get the lead role in a camp play.
Was it possible that she could actually have fun at camp?

ISBN 0-590-40375-3/$2.25 US/$2.95 CAN

AMY AND LAURA
Marilyn Sachs

Would Laura really report her own sister—
to the teacher?

Laura's always looked out for her little sister Amy. She's
protected Amy from bullies and helped her with her
homework. Now that Laura has a job at school as a hall
monitor, things are changing. She has to treat her sister like
all the other kids, doesn't she? That's not what their mother
and father think!

ISBN 0-590-40529-2/$2.50 US/$3.50 CAN

UNDERDOG
Marilyn Sachs

Izzy Cummings is all alone.

When Izzy's father dies, Izzy is sent out to California to stay with an aunt and uncle she's never met. But Izzy doesn't fit into their sophisticated lives; they're just too busy for a quiet, lonely niece. Izzy feels like the biggest underdog in the whole world.

Then Izzy finds a picture of Gus, the little black dog that belonged to her family when she was little. Whatever happened to Gus? Izzy has to know—even if it means skipping school and disobeying her aunt to find out. She and Gus are two underdogs…and they belong together.

ISBN 0-590-40406-7/$2.50 US/$3.50 CAN

THE HOT
AND COLD SUMMER
Johanna Hurwitz

Crazy things start to happen when Bolivia comes to town!

Rory and Derek are best friends forever. . . . At least that's what they think — until they meet Bolivia. She's visiting next door all summer and everyone wants the three of them to be buddies. But since she's a *girl*, Rory and Derek decide to ignore her completely. Except it's not so easy to ignore someone who has her own pet parrot and who likes to make snowballs — out of ice-cream!

Derek starts thinking Bolivia's the funniest, craziest kid he's ever met, but Rory still says three's a crowd. Is there room in their friendship for Bolivia, or is she about to break up a perfect team?

ISBN 0-590-40722-8/$2.50 US/$3.50 CAN

Delicious New Apples®

Exciting Series for You!

ANIMAL INN™ by Virginia Vail

When 13-year-old Val Taylor comes home from school, she spends her afternoons with a menagerie of horses, dogs, and cats–the residents of Animal Inn, her dad's veterinary clinic.

PETS ARE FOR KEEPS #1	**$2.50 / $3.50 Can.**
A KID'S BEST FRIEND #2	**$2.50 / $3.50 Can.**
MONKEY BUSINESS #3	**$2.50 / $3.50 Can.**

THE BABY-SITTERS CLUB™ by Ann M. Martin

Meet Kristy, Claudia, Mary Anne, and Stacey...the four members of the Baby-sitters Club! They're 7th graders who get involved in all kinds of adventures–with school, boys, and, of course, baby-sitting!

FREE
Baby-sitters Kit!
Details in Books 1, 2, and 3

KRISTY'S GREAT IDEA #1	**$2.50 / $3.50 Can.**
CLAUDIA AND THE PHANTOM PHONE CALLS #2	**$2.50 / $3.50 Can.**
THE TRUTH ABOUT STACEY #3	**$2.50 / $3.50 Can.**
MARY ANNE SAVES THE DAY #4	**$2.50 / $3.50 Can.**

APPLE® CLASSICS

Kids everywhere have loved these stories for a long time...and so will you!

THE CALL OF THE WILD by Jack London
After being stolen from his home, Buck–part St. Bernard, part German Shepherd–returns to the wild...as the leader of a wolf pack! **$2.50 / $3.95 Can.**

LITTLE WOMEN by Louisa May Alcott (abridged)
The March sisters were more than just sisters–they were friends! You'll never forget Meg, Jo, Beth, and Amy. **$2.50 / $3.95 Can.**

WHITE FANG by Jack London
White Fang–half dog, half wolf–is captured by the Indians, tortured by a cowardly man, and he becomes a fierce, deadly fighter. Will he ever find a loving master? **$2.50 / $3.50 Can.**

Look in your bookstores now for these great titles!

Scholastic Books

APP871